Just Past TWO

COMES IN THREES SERIES

Just Past TWO

COMES IN THREES SERIES

ELIA WINTERS

Entangled Publishing, LLC
2614 South Timberline Road
Suite 105, PMB 159
Fort Collins, CO 80525
rights@entangledpublishing.com

Scorched is an imprint of Entangled Publishing, LLC.

Edited by Heather Howland
Cover design by Mayhem Cover Creations
Cover photography by 4 PM production/Shutterstock

Manufactured in the United States of America

First Edition May 2019

entangled
scorched

For the A-Team

Chapter One

Abby stared up at the Hotel Mapleton through the windshield. Her husband Sam had the car still idling, the heater blasting warm air against their feet, while outside, a light sprinkling of snow coated everything in a frosted glaze. Except for the noises of the car, silence surrounded them, giving Abby ample time to have second thoughts.

"You know, we don't have to go."

She looked over at Sam, who had just said what she was thinking. Always the picture of practicality, he shrugged and fixed her with his best "It's only logical" face. It was one of his most common expressions. He smiled, the smile he gave when he was trying to be supportive, another common expression. She'd been looking at this face for ten years now, through three years of dating and seven years of marriage, and the variety of expressions was as familiar as his face itself.

"I know we don't." She looked back up at the hotel, where her ten-year college reunion was presumably already underway. Their breath was beginning to fog the windows, even with the heater on, softening the edges of the resplendent building. Still decked out for the holidays, the hotel glistened with white twinkle lights beneath a glaze of snow. Even looking like every New England Christmas photograph, though, its beauty didn't assuage any of the anxiety tightening her stomach.

Sam gave her hand a reassuring squeeze, his black leather driving gloves slick against the softness of her palm. "We can always go back home. Spend New Year's on our own, no reunion, no small talk, no explaining to hundreds of people what you've been up to for the past ten years."

Abby swallowed. That would be easy, wouldn't it? The thought had a certain appeal. She'd become a different person in these last ten years, and not by accident. Bringing Sam into this environment was already merging two worlds never designed to intersect. Did she even *want* to be here? She'd agonized about it when the invitation first came in the mail, accompanied by a flood of old memories, and had eventually decided yes. She'd had reasons.

"The car's not even off," Sam added. "I could just put it back in drive."

Abby started to laugh. "You know, if *you* don't want to go, you could just say that."

"Hey, I don't mind." Sam put his hands up in a defensive gesture. "I'm happy to go. I'm just saying, you have options."

"I know. I know I have options." The choice was hers, obviously.   `

"I'm looking forward to it, to tell you the truth." Sam rubbed his chin, contemplative. "A glimpse of college Abby? It's like spotting a rare bird."

Abby snorted. "A dodo, maybe."

"An extinct bird?" Sam gaped comically. "That's even more remarkable."

Laughing, Abby shoved him. "You know what I mean. I was kind of a dumbass back then." She twined her fingers together in her lap.

"You? Never." Sam's warm smile was too open, not a trace of guile in sight. He really believed this, too. He believed there was no way Abby could be other than the person she was now: mature, respectable Abby Wood Burke, who could have fun but would never go too far. A woman with class, who could be playful but would never be too raunchy, a woman with a good head on her shoulders.

Basically, the opposite of everything she was back in college.

If they left and went home now, Sam would know her only as the woman she'd worked so hard to be, not as the wild young woman she once was. Sure, he'd had hints of it: he knew she'd had a number of past relationships, for example, but she'd been mum about specifics. Her wild dating history was too wrapped up in the rest of the person she'd been, the person who'd almost ruined her life with careless bad decisions, and she was content to forget those embarrassing memories. Leaving now meant she could keep those secrets for good.

But damn, she'd lost touch with too many people since college, had forgotten too many friendships that might deserve rekindling. She'd been thinking about this reunion ever since they announced it last spring, watched the photos pop up on the Facebook event page, and RSVP'd to that invitation when it had arrived. She'd already weighed the pros and cons. Sam loved her, and he wasn't going to judge her for her past. She'd made something of herself, had grown up into a respectable woman with a gorgeous, brilliant husband and a successful career. She'd bought a beautiful green dress that highlighted her eyes and the fullness of her curves. She was not about to turn her back on this. Abby Wood never backed down from a challenge, and even now that she was Abby Wood Burke, that quality still remained.

Abby tossed her long red curls back over her shoulder and unfastened her seat belt. "Shut the car off, babe. There's an open bar with our name on it."

The main ballroom of the Hotel Mapleton was already crowded, people spilling out into the foyers, laughing and talking loud enough to be heard over the music blasting from inside. The faces were almost familiar, one step past where she could place them, people from her classes who had been acquaintances but not friends. Then, like a picture coming into focus, she started identifying people she'd known well. Students from her dorm, from her art classes, from the clubs she'd joined, one after another everywhere she looked.

"Holy shit, this takes me back." She grabbed Sam's arm. He steadied her, like he always steadied her.

"See some people you know?"

"So many." She scanned the crowd again. "I'm just trying to think of who you need to meet first."

Sam nudged her. "I think you've been spotted." He gestured to where two guys were rushing over to meet them from across the room.

Phil and James looked so much like their college selves, she could have picked them out anywhere. Phil was still as tall and big as ever, built like a refrigerator and almost as white, carrying a few extra pounds and sporting some glasses but with the same football player body underneath. And James, at Phil's side, skin flushed pink with probably too much alcohol, looked as proud to be on Phil's arm as he had the day they'd started dating senior year. He'd cut his hair shorter since then, the curls trimmed down to a manageable length, but otherwise he had the same baby face despite being ten years older.

Phil wrapped Abby up in an embrace that squeezed the air out of her, pulling her away from Sam as he did so. "Holy shit. I can't believe this." Phil held her at arm's length and looked her up and down, grinning. "Abby Wood. Stunning as ever. Is it still Abby Wood?" He looked over at Sam.

"There's a Burke on there now." She stepped back and introduced the two. "Phil, this is my husband Sam Burke. Sam, this is Phil Smith and James… I'm sorry, I'm drawing a blank on your last name."

"Peterson," James supplied, shaking hands. "Your wife and my husband were roommates way back when."

"Roommates for one disastrous semester." Phil laughed uproariously. "Shit, what a bad idea that was! Your wife here almost got me kicked off the football team. Remember that, Abby? The night of the streaking? When the police came?"

Eyebrows raised, Sam looked to Abby for an explanation. "What?"

"No. Really?" She grasped for the memory through the annals of the past. She'd had so many encounters with campus security and the local police, they all ran together. "I swear, I don't remember that."

"Hand to God." Phil elbowed James. "This was before you knew me. This girl holds a raging kegger during finals week. Our apartment is barely a block from the edge of campus. Middle of the party, she convinces me to go streaking."

"Wait. Wait a minute." Abby shook her head. The details were starting to come back. "If I remember, you didn't take much convincing. You were always halfway naked at any given time."

Phil paused. "Okay, true. True. But you definitely put me up to it, saying you'd do it if I would."

Oh, shit. It was *this* story. Abby started to hold up a hand to stop him, but Phil just kept going. "So you go, run butt-ass naked through the center of campus and back, everybody loves it, right? I mean, obviously. And I get literally one block from our home and the cops pull up, arrest me. Coach was furious. I spent the next two weeks running suicides."

Phil was already laughing before the end of his story, and James joined in along with Sam, leaving Abby standing there chuckling. Ah, shit, that wasn't exactly the way she'd wanted to open this reunion. They were supposed to ease in with some of the less disastrous stories, not her running bare-ass naked through campus.

Sam wrapped an arm around her waist and gave her a squeeze. "You never told me this. Streaking on campus?"

"That's not even the half of it." Phil shook his head. "We should get drinks. Come on, James, give me a hand. What can I grab for you two?"

"Um. Wine? Whatever red they have. Thanks." Abby looked to Sam, who asked for the same.

"Wine?" Phil shook his head. "Damn, things really do change, don't they?"

He disappeared a moment later toward the bar with their drink order, leaving them alone, and Abby exhaled shakily. "Okay, so, you might get your wish for some stories about me."

"Yeah, I'm picking up on that." Sam grinned, his expression teasing and not at all upset. Thank God. He managed to always look so put together, with his wavy dark hair and perfect jawline, clean-shaven for the occasion, filling out a slim-cut suit with only a hint of those beautiful, lean CrossFit muscles. He cleaned up like a GQ advertisement. This wasn't the kind of man who probably went streaking in college, or who dated a few dozen people in a long string of short-term relationships that never went anywhere, or who had nearly flunked out of college by being an irresponsible fuckup. She knew Sam's past. He was the valedictorian of his high school class, studied architecture at Cornell on a near full ride, and was now a star architect in his firm. He was settled, professional, brilliant, and for some reason that occasionally eluded her, madly in love with her, and they'd somehow ended up in a romance and marriage that was—without a doubt—the best thing to ever happen to her.

"Hey." Sam shook her by the shoulders. "You tuning out on me? Earth to Abby."

"I'm sorry." Abby flashed him her best flirtatious grin. "I was just thinking how gorgeous you are."

Sam rolled his eyes. "Yeah, a likely story. Probably thinking of more of your college adventures that you've been keeping from me." He waggled his eyebrows.

"For your own good, I swear." Abby gestured to the buffet. "I think you're in for the long haul of stories about me getting into trouble. You want to go get some food to go with these drinks?"

Sam laughed. "You're damn right I do."

They brought plates of finger foods over to a table with Phil and James. She obviously wanted to see more people at this reunion than just those two, but they were a nice place to start, since Phil had been a good friend on and off throughout her years at school. At least most of the stories Phil could tell would be stories about parties. He was gay, so they'd never slept together, and hopefully they could avoid that entire realm of Abby's past altogether.

Phil handed a glass of wine to each of them. "So tell me about yourself, Sam. What do you do? How did you and Abby meet? How long have you been married?"

"Babe." James put a hand on Phil's arm. "Give it a rest, all right? Let them get a word in edgewise."

"I'm an architect at Dooney, right here in Mapleton." Sam sipped his wine. He looked totally at ease here, even though he didn't know a single person, and Abby could fall in love with him all over again. "Abby and I met at a pottery class she was teaching at the community center. It turns out I'm shit at pottery, but I had the hots for the teacher, and we've been together ever since. Married seven years this coming April."

"You do pottery?" James asked Abby.

Phil tapped his finger on the table, looking like the memories were slowly coming back. "Yeah, you were an art major, right?"

"Still doing pottery. Just as a hobby now, though. Not really interested in making a living at it. Finest way to ruin a hobby is to turn it into a job." Abby had definitely sat at that crossroads for a while after her junior year internship, looking at an art degree in a field that she had been slowly starting to hate. "I switched majors, and now I'm an MRI tech. Learned to love art again when I didn't have to do it full time." She raised her glass in a toast. "You two have been together since college?"

"Straight through. Ten years now." Phil made love eyes at James, which was adorable. "We got married basically right out of college."

"And, great news." James pulled out his phone, tongue poking out the side of his mouth in concentration as he scrolled through pictures. He triumphantly turned his phone around to show them a photo of a toddler, all large blue eyes and too much curly hair. "This is Liam. We've just been approved to adopt him."

They cooed over the adorable baby, and that shifted the conversation more to James and Phil, their jobs, their struggles buying a house, the minutiae of life going from age twenty-two to thirty-two as they grew into full adulthood. She'd grown into full adulthood, too, mostly by cutting ties with her college self and starting anew with Sam, and sitting here bridged the divide in a weird way. As conversation waned, their plates emptied, and finally Abby turned to Sam.

"I love this song. Do you want to dance?"

Sam knew she didn't love this song, but he could also take a hint, so with a cordial goodbye to Phil and James, they made their way out to the dance floor, and he swept her smoothly into his arms.

They didn't go dancing often enough. They'd gone a lot in the beginning of their relationship, when they were younger and searching for any signs of nightlife in and around small-town Mapleton. Dancing to house music, ballroom, salsa, they'd gone wherever they could find a steady beat and a lively crowd. But life became ever busier, and dancing—like many things—faded over time. His body pressed against hers conjured up all kinds of memories from their younger years.

"So why am I really dancing with you?" he asked. "I thought you liked those guys."

She smiled. Sam was clearly not fooled. "I did. I do." Back at the table, Phil and James were already in conversation with someone else. "I just wanted some space."

Sam turned and dipped her easily, guiding her through a samba that somehow fit perfectly to this pop ballad. "You worried I'm going to keep finding out more about this bare-ass running career of yours?"

Abby tipped her head forward onto Sam's chest and started laughing, her voice muffled against his shirt. "I can't believe that came up. I swear to God, I haven't done that lately."

Sam squeezed her hand, prompting her to look up again. "We all change. I think that's pretty normal." His voice, low and smooth, soothed whatever nerves had cropped up during the conversation. The man didn't have a dishonest bone in his body. He was a man of convictions and principles, but he could identify guile in anyone else, and especially in her. "Is this kind of stuff the reason you never talk much about college?"

"You know the important things. You know I dated a lot, that I wasn't ready to settle down, and that all changed when I met you." Everything he needed to know, really, and he'd never pried.

"Babe, you know I don't care what you got up to in college." He twirled her around once, surprising her into more laughter, and pulled her back to him again. "I love the person you are now. It doesn't matter who you were back then."

"Easy for you to say. You were a Boy Scout."

Sam's expression turned serious, but the kind of serious that was comical in its intensity. He even stopped dancing, holding her at arm's length. "Abby Wood Burke, I need to know this right now. Back in college, did you kill a man?"

Abby burst out laughing, heart suddenly full. He could always make her laugh. "I did. That's what I've been keeping from you."

"I knew it." He shook his head in disappointment. "You going to prison is really going to put a damper on this New Year's." He dropped a chaste kiss on her lips before sweeping her into the dance again. This was textbook for Sam; he wasn't a PDA kind of guy, and for all his jokes, he was pretty serious underneath. She loved that about him. She'd been drawn to his seriousness from the very beginning. Even when they were first dating, he'd been so respectful of her, never wanting to push her boundaries, until she'd practically had to drag him to bed. She'd landed herself one of the good ones. It had all felt so tentative back then, a relationship with someone she could see a future with, back when she was still trying to muddle her way into adulthood.

Over Sam's shoulder, the crowd parted, and another familiar face came into view. She froze, body going suddenly motionless like she couldn't convince it to move. She must have gone pale, because Sam's response was all concern. "What? Are you okay?"

Across the dance floor, a familiar figure strolled out of the crowd. His name and a score of memories both came flooding back all at once. Zachary Levine, tall and bronze, always leaving conversations half finished because of swim team practice or a lifeguarding gig. Zach, who she'd never fucked but had wanted to, Zach of so many near misses, privy to all her wildest days.

He looked just as good as he had back in college. He was still tall and golden brown, with light hair that probably still lightened up in the summer. He still had that swimmer's long, lean body with an impossibly broad smile, and wild curly hair that spoke to his biracial ethnicity. He even had freckles like her, darker constellations scattered across his skin. He made eye contact with her across the crowded dance floor and started coming their way.

Abby looked to Sam, like he might somehow be able to help, which was ridiculous. "It's Zach," she said, like that would explain anything at all.

His eyebrows went up even more. "Okay? You know I don't know who the hell any of these people are."

"Zachary Levine. He was on my floor back in freshman and sophomore year. He dated my roommate for a while, and then he…" She trailed off as he closed the distance, all warm smiles that brought up the same giddy nervousness of her youth.

"Abby Wood!"

Abby stepped out of Sam's embrace, and Zach swept her up into a hug, already laughing, his body so warm against hers. He still smelled the same, kind of, and she didn't even know she'd remember his scent until she was breathing it in. Zach held her at arm's length, looking her up and down. "Holy shit, Abby, you look amazing. It can't have been ten years. You look as young as when we graduated."

"It's been ten years." She gestured to her husband, fumbling her words. "This is Zach. Sam. This is Sam, my husband." She moved her arm up and down, like a high-speed Vanna White showing off the latest prize puzzle. "Sam, this is Zachary Levine. We were friends back in college."

Zach shook Sam's hand, warm and cordial. "You lucky bastard. I didn't think anyone could get Abby to settle down."

"Me?" Like hell she was going to take that slander. "You dated pretty much the whole floor!" She turned to Sam. "Listen. I may have had my own wild days in college, but Zach puts them to shame."

"Oh really?" Sam grinned, probably happy he was going to get these wild tales after all. "Come on, Zach, maybe you can tell me some stories. Abby keeps dragging me away from everyone who might be able to dish the dirt."

Zach's laugh, loud and free like it always had been, took her right back to the crush she'd nursed for him for years. They were always passing like ships in the night, Zach moving from relationship to relationship, never single at the same time she was. "Let's grab a table and a drink."

Zach left for the bar, and Abby grabbed Sam's arm. "Come on. Go easy on me."

"Okay, okay, I'm not gonna pump him for information." Sam held up three fingers. "Scout's honor."

"Fine. One drink." She pulled him toward the bar after Zach. "And if I ask you to dance again, we go."

• • •

Abby was pretty jumpy tonight. It was just a reunion, and she'd been looking forward to going, or so Sam had thought. But ever since they'd gotten here, she'd vacillated between loud and shy, shifting from the composed, put-together, brilliant woman he loved, to some kind of unrecognizable version of herself, in turns raucous and uncertain, trying out different emotions like shoes.

Now, though, three drinks into an increasingly laughter-filled conversation with Zach, she was back to the confident self he'd remembered. They hadn't actually told any stories of the past yet, just stuff about their current lives. Zach told them about his years in the Coast Guard, living down in Florida, and moving back to the area just last year.

"Western Mass, can't stay away." Zach shrugged. "My company offered me a relocation deal too good to pass up. I'm on the road almost a hundred nights a year, but I don't mind."

"The hospitality industry suits you," Abby said with a smile. "You certainly seemed hospitable enough to our entire dorm."

Zach threw back his head and laughed. "Okay, that's fair, that's fair."

Sam still couldn't tell if Abby had slept with Zach. He wasn't going to ask, not yet, anyway, but couldn't stop the curiosity. It wasn't jealousy. It was something else, something totally different from jealousy, something he couldn't quite put his finger on. Zach was a handsome man, and thinking of him with Abby, for some reason, wasn't unpleasant at all. Maybe he'd secretly been hoping the stories would go there, a tantalizing hint of a wild Abby hidden inside the familiar Abby he loved.

They moved on to talking about Sam's career, and then how he and Abby had met. She told the story better than he did, about him losing control of his vase in the middle of the class and hitting her with a chunk of clay just as she was coming over to compliment him on his progress. It was a funny story, one he didn't mind even though he came off looking a little silly, and hearing Abby tell it was always a delight.

Zach laughed. "Did you tell him it would take a few more drinks to get you into mud wrestling?"

Abby wobbled her wine and snorted. "I did not."

Zach put a hand to his head. "Do you remember that

time?"

"What time?" Abby giggled.

"Mud wrestling in the quad for the Orchard Games. Freshman, sophomore year?"

Abby held up her glass. "I was motherfucking Orchard Mud Champion. Of course I remember." She toasted herself and drank.

"You mud wrestled?" Sam stared, trying to wrap his mind around it. Mud wrestling? Who actually did that? Abby, apparently. His Abby. Sure, she was playful, but that… was a whole different level of playful.

Zach jumped in before she could answer. "You should have seen it. She was like an Olympian." He paused, expression going thoughtful. "Your hair was blue back then, right?"

"Blue?" Sam turned more fully in his chair. He couldn't picture Abby without her long, beautiful red hair.

"Don't remind me." She finished her glass of wine. "Bleaching it almost ruined it. Part of my wild, rebellious phase."

"You mean, the one that lasted all four years of college?" Zach teased, nudging her with his elbow.

"Please." Abby threw her napkin at Zach, but her smile wobbled a little. "Don't exaggerate."

"You should be proud of your legacy." Zach's expression was earnest. "I think you're the only person to accomplish the full Campus Twenty."

Abby's normally pale skin went white, her freckles standing out even more, and she covered her face with her hands. "Oh God."

Sam shouldn't ask. She was clearly embarrassed, but underneath her hands, was she…laughing? She pulled her hands away, and yeah, she was laughing even as her pale skin flushed red.

So he had to ask. "What's the Campus Twenty?"

Zach raised an eyebrow to Abby. "You want to tell him?"

Abby tipped her head back to stare up at the ceiling of the ballroom, then looked over to Sam and said the next words all in a rush. "Twenty public spots on campus to fool around without getting caught."

"Oh."

What was he supposed to say, other than "oh"? So she'd fooled around in public before. That wasn't even such a big deal. It wasn't something *he* had ever done, but Abby was always more adventurous than him. It wasn't like that was a surprise. He'd followed the straight and narrow all the way through college, and she'd had some…indiscretions.

"It wasn't anything," Abby insisted. "Just some hand jobs, maybe a blow job, some stupid shit we did when we were young and dumb."

Zach raised his glass to her, then looked her up and down once more. What must Abby look like through his eyes? All soft curves, the plunging neckline of her dress revealing the generous swell of her breasts, as tantalizing as she had been ten years ago. "Well, not *we*," he clarified. "Not you and me."

Zach and Abby hadn't slept together. For some reason, that disappointed Sam, which was weird. He could nearly picture it, though. Abby and Zach, laughing together, getting caught up in breathless kisses, fooling around somewhere on campus where they might get caught…

It was enough to get him half hard, an unexpected reaction. He wanted to know more. "So you hit all twenty?"

"Yes. I hit all twenty." She sounded resigned. "But really, I'm not that girl anymore."

"It's nothing to be ashamed of, you know." Sam tried to choose his words carefully. "I think it's funny." Not funny, but arousing, and yet he couldn't say that with Zach right here listening. Could he even say it at all? How would Abby receive that? She wasn't the type to kiss and tell, and this line of conversation was clearly making her a little uncomfortable. They should probably change the subject.

"Yeah. Funny." Abby drained her glass of wine.

Zach looked past them. "Shit, is that Heather? I haven't seen her in forever." He put his hand over Abby's. "I've gotta run. It's been so good to see you. Look me up sometime, okay? I'd love to get together." He squeezed her hand, then shook Sam's. "Great meeting you, Sam. We'll have to talk soon." He left Abby and Sam alone at the table with the silence left in his absence.

"You know, I really don't mind it," Sam said after another awkward moment of silence.

"Do you know what my nickname was back in college?" Abby ran a finger around the lip of her empty wineglass. She didn't wait for him to answer. "Abby Wood If She Could. Because of stuff like that. Mud wrestling. Dyeing my hair. Streaking. The Campus Twenty. I was the girl who would do anything. How do you *really* feel about that?"

"Curious?"

Abby rolled her eyes. "You don't have to placate me, Sam."

"I just want to know why you never told me." He couldn't keep the hurt tone out of his voice, even though it was slight.

"Because the past is the past. I'm not that person anymore."

She'd been saying that all night, insisting that she'd changed, and clearly she had. Over the almost ten years they'd been together, he'd never seen any sign of this wild woman from college. "Why aren't you that person anymore?"

That clearly wasn't the question she'd been expecting, and she stared at him before averting her eyes. "I grew out of it."

"All at once?"

Her expression grew somber. "I knew it was time to change when that hit man came after me."

Sam stared at her, not sure *what* to believe, until Abby cracked up laughing. He joined her, the tension easing. Okay, so she didn't want to explain further. He held out his hand. "Come on. You want to dance?"

Abby got to her feet, wobbly, and grabbed at him for support. "Whoa. All that wine just hit me at once."

Sam slid an arm around her waist. "I don't know how you walk in those heels."

"It's fashion." She smiled up at him, her smile kind of lazy, the way she always got with a bit of wine in her. "Maybe I should get some air instead. You want to get some fresh air with me?"

"It's below freezing out there."

"We'll get our coats. Come on." She tugged him toward the hall.

Even with his coat on, it was damn freezing outside, and he stayed close to Abby as they walked out onto the big back deck of the hotel. The deck was clearly not used often in winter, snow blown loosely against the wall behind them, large potted evergreens looming dark instead of wrapped in twinkle lights like the rest of the decor on the building. With only the light filtering through the window and nothing but darkness in the field behind, everything was a mass of shadows. Abby walked over to the corner and gripped the wooden railing, seeming unbothered by the cold, and stared out into the deepness of the night. The music was still audible out here, a muted pulse in the otherwise silent evening.

They both turned as the door burst open and a couple came tumbling out, laughing, already in the clinch of an embrace. They didn't even check for other people, lips meeting, hands sliding over bodies. Abby and Sam, as one, both moved deeper into the shadows of the building.

Abby grabbed Sam's arm, speaking just loud enough that he could hear. "We should go."

"We can't. They're right in front of the door." He pulled her closer back against him, her body tight in front of his as they tried to shrink back into the shadows against the building.

The other couple stood less than fifteen feet away, kissing as if they couldn't get enough of each other. They shifted slightly, leaning against the railing, and a shaft of light from the window fell across the man's face. Abby's whole body went taut. It was Zach. Zach was out here with a woman from the party, a woman who was slipping her hands down into his pants.

It was definitely too late to escape now. If they gave themselves away, Zach and his partner were going to ask why they didn't reveal themselves sooner. The only answer, that they were peeping from the shadows like perverts, wasn't going to go over well. Fortunately, Zach and his partner were making enough noise to hide other sounds.

"Fuck, Heather."

Heather laughed, deep and throaty, leaning in for another kiss. "Haven't gotten my hands on you since college. Just like old times, huh?"

"Shh. Keep it down." Zach was smiling as he spoke. "We're gonna get caught."

All along the front of Sam's body, Abby's curves pressed warm and soft against him. Something about her closeness, the tension of the moment, the heat of what they were watching, and he was fully hard before he felt it happening. Abby shifted, hips pressing against his cock, and then froze.

They'd been drinking, and hell, it was New Year's, and he'd been having naughty thoughts all night. Maybe he could indulge them, just a little bit. He leaned down to whisper in her ear. "It's hot, isn't it?"

Abby hesitated before nodding.

Her breasts were so close to his hand. He'd never do something like this normally, never risk getting caught, but the blood thundering in his body obscured other thought.

Abby gasped as Sam cupped her full, round breast, the sound drowned out by another of Zach's moans. Then she pressed even farther in to his hand. Damn. Pulse racing, cock already throbbing, he slid his hand under the deep neckline of her dress and found the hard peak of her nipple beneath the flimsy material of her bra.

"Sam," she whispered.

"Shh." He rolled the tip between his fingers, making her shiver. "Doesn't it make you hot?"

She paused, and then slowly nodded again. He was harder and more turned on than he could remember being before, and all he was doing was playing lightly with her nipple. Of course, they were in public, watching another couple fooling around right in front of them, and they'd certainly never been in this situation before.

Zach lifted Heather onto the railing of the deck, and Abby shivered. Heather giggled loudly. "It's freezing!"

Zach kissed her again, moving between her legs, and Heather's giggles switched to moans. Zach fumbled around with something in his pocket, then he heard the telltale sound of a condom wrapper. Had Sam ever watched someone have sex before? No, actually. He wasn't even that into porn, because it was all so fake. This, though? This was totally different. Zach shifted forward into the cradle of Heather's thighs, and she moaned low and breathlessly as he slid into her.

Sam was going to combust right here. Even with the freezing temperatures, sweat beaded on his forehead. One hand still cupping her breast, he reached the other down, under the hem of Abby's skirt, trailing his fingers up along the inside of her thighs. This was too far, too risky, too much, and she was going to stop him any minute now, surely...

Instead, Abby moved her legs farther apart, granting permission. He brushed the top of stockings, then bare skin, acres of bare skin, and instead of the line of her panties…the soft, slick wetness of her pussy.

She wasn't wearing underwear. He couldn't even question it, because his hand was right where he wanted it to be, and he dipped into her hot, wet heat to find the bud of her clit nestled among all that softness.

Abby shuddered in his arms. "*Sam*," she breathed, but it wasn't a protest, something broken and desperate in her whisper. Jesus. He'd never heard her sound like that. The space was snug, her thighs tight around his hand, and she was so damn wet already. She'd gotten wet watching them.

"I like watching this," he whispered again into her ear. And maybe this was too far, but he was going to say it anyway. "I like imagining you like that."

She swore under her breath, wobbling in his arms, and he held her tighter against him as he fingered her clit. "Does this make you hot?" He needed to hear her say it, needed to know it wasn't just him.

"Yes." She leaned back against him, letting him support her, her head resting heavily on his collarbone. "God, Sam, what if we get caught?"

He nipped her earlobe. She was absolutely drenching his fingers. Leaning a bit farther forward, he could reach deeper, moving past her clit to curl two fingers into her welcoming pussy. If only it could be his dick right now, fucking into her the way Zach was fucking into Heather: short, blunt thrusts that had her moaning. This would have to do, the heel of his hand grinding into her clit. "We're not gonna get caught. Unless you like the idea of that."

She shuddered again. Maybe he was onto something. "You like that, don't you?" He didn't need to ask. "You like the thought of someone seeing us."

"Don't be silly." Abby's voice was still barely audible, a whisper, but he knew this woman. He knew when she was lying, and the scenario started spilling from his mouth before he even knew what he was saying.

"Imagine someone watching us the way we're watching them. You like that? You think of that, all those times when you were fooling around on campus? Hmm? You think about being watched?"

Pressed against him, Abby began to tremble, her pussy tightening impossibly on his fingers. She never came this easily, but here on the freezing cold deck watching someone else have sex, she was already on the edge, already rocking her hips minutely against his hand.

"I want you to come, just like this." He ground his palm harder into her sensitive flesh, rewarded by the tiny moan she let slip. "Shh. No sounds. Don't let them hear us. Come on my hand, beautiful."

She gripped the arm he had wrapped around her, fingernails digging into his skin. And with a sudden, nearly imperceptible intake of breath, she came, her muscles rippling around his fingers. His cock throbbed in his pants, aching for release, aching for her touch, but he could forget all of that in the incredible feeling of making her come on his fingers.

In the fog of Abby's climax, Sam could hear Zach murmuring to Heather. "That's it, gorgeous. Just like that. I want to feel you come."

Heather was less reserved, her voice regular volume as she swore and prayed and repeated his name. Just as Heather seized up and cried out, Abby sagged in Sam's arms, her climax ebbing.

Sam carefully slid his fingers out of Abby's wet folds and up to his mouth. She turned in his arms in time to see him suck her juices off his fingers, and in the dim light, her eyes went wide and her mouth opened slightly. She stepped in to him and kissed him, kissing her own taste from his mouth. Then, without other preamble, she dropped down to her knees and unzipped his pants.

He'd never gotten a blow job in public before. No fumbling foreplay in the backseat of his car, no clandestine fooling around in college. Now, though, Abby was wrapping her hot, wet mouth all the way down his length while just beyond their shadowy alcove, Zach was finishing with a low groan inside Heather. Abby moved like a woman possessed, swallowing him down. She'd never sucked him off like this, never with this kind of fervor. This was all new. What else had he been missing? What else was she hiding from him, and why?

He couldn't even warn her before he was coming. Climax ripped through him, pleasure like a punch in the gut. He bit his knuckles to stay silent, emptying himself down Abby's throat. She sucked and sucked, swallowing, not missing a drop, and he grabbed at the wall of the building to steady himself. Dimly, he heard Zach and Heather laughing, saw the fumbled recovery of their post-coital encounter, closing his eyes at last as the door back inside slammed shut behind them.

"Fuck." He finally said it at full volume, his dick softening in Abby's warm mouth. She got to her feet, looking way too satisfied with herself. God, he loved her. He leaned in to kiss her, tasting them both. "What the hell," he breathed.

She tucked him back into his pants and zipped them up. "What got into you?" she asked, her smile tentative.

What got into him? What about her? "Just...caught up in the moment, I guess."

"Right." She licked her lips. "Do I look like a whore?"

I'd like it if you did. The thought came to mind immediately, shockingly, and he pushed it away. "Of course not."

"C'mon." She gestured to the door. "It's fucking freezing out here. Let's go dance."

Chapter Two

"And...you just haven't brought it up since then?" Abby's best friend Angela frowned at her, pausing in front of an endless row of pipe fixtures. "You fool around on the porch at the reunion while literally watching somebody else fuck, and then you go home and go to bed and don't talk about it again?"

Having a conversation about her relationship in the middle of a Home Depot was weird, but it's where they always ended up on one of Angela's home improvement adventures. Now, though, watching Angela give her side-eye while surrounded by towering shelving and repair tools, Abby's mouth went dry.

"I don't know if I want to have this conversation right now." She looked around. "Maybe I shouldn't have brought it up. It doesn't seem appropriate here."

Angela wheeled her cart farther down the aisle and waved off another well-meaning employee coming by to ask if she needed help. With her blonde hair tied up in a messy bun and a pink fuzzy sweater over a willowy build, Angela was often mistaken as someone who didn't know what she was doing in a home improvement store. Little did they know Angela was here almost as much as someone who worked here, what with a new project popping up nearly every weekend. "It's a Home Depot, Abby, not a library. Tell me more. Like why you might suddenly have crazy hot public sex with your husband, the same husband you describe as 'stable, predictable, boring'—"

"I never called him boring," Abby interrupted. "You make me sound like I hate all the mature things about him. Sam is *not* boring. I love him."

Angela rolled her eyes. "Yeah, I know you love him. You've been together for what, almost a decade now? And super lovey and gross, all the time. I get it." When Abby went to interrupt, she held up a hand. "But listen. *Listen.* You have to admit this is a little out of character for him, and to just go home and not talk about it at all? You haven't been curious about what's up?"

"I didn't want to ask." In fact, Abby had spent the last two days justifying to herself all the reasons they didn't need to talk about it. "But it was New Year's. Don't people always get a little crazy on New Year's?"

"Does Sam usually get crazy on New Year's?"

Abby hesitated. "Well…no, not usually." Not ever.

Angela gave her a "You see what I mean?" face, which Abby ignored to press onward in her defense. "But also, we'd been drinking. And reunions are kind of weird, too."

"Liminal spaces." Angela nodded knowingly.

"What?"

"Liminal spaces. Somebody was talking about them at work last week, and I looked them up. They're transitional spaces that seem to exist outside of space and time. Like playgrounds at night. Or airports. Or pretty much any Target." Angela consulted her tiny spiral notebook, then steered her cart toward pipe fixtures while Abby hustled to keep up. "Reunions are weird because it's a set of people all in a place where you're not used to seeing them."

"Right! So maybe, with New Year's, and the fact that it was a reunion, Sam was just acting weird."

Angela consulted the list in her notebook again, then tossed a few elbow connectors into the cart. "I don't think it counts if it's not his reunion. You see pipe dope around here?" She scanned the aisle. "Oh, there it is."

Abby trailed after her. "I've been trying to convince myself this is a fluke."

"Do you want it to be a fluke?"

Abby hesitated, and Angela stopped her cart and leaned on it to ask another question. "Do you want to go anywhere with this?"

"Like where?"

"Well, like spicing up your marriage, for one." Angela shrugged a shoulder. "If he was into it, and you're saying he *was* into it, then maybe this is an opportunity to go a little further. Go wild." She waved jazz hands.

Go wild. What even would going wild look like with Sam? "I don't think that's in the cards for us."

Angela smiled. "Because Sam's a tight-ass?"

"He's not a tight-ass." Abby threw two giant boxes of humidifier filters into Angela's cart as revenge. "He's stable. He's professional. He's loving. He's considerate." She ticked off his qualities on her fingers. "He's perfect for me. He's everything I need."

Angela put the boxes of filters back on the shelf. "Is he everything you want, though?"

"Of course."

Angela blew a loose strand of hair off her face. "Abby, I've known you for a long-ass time. Including during college. I let you sleep on my couch for a month when you got kicked out of campus housing." Abby winced, but Angela kept talking. "And you told me, you said, 'Angela, I'm gonna turn everything around,' and you did. Cold turkey. Stopped partying, stopped going out, stopped doing everything you enjoyed."

"Stopped flunking out of college, you mean." Easy for Angela to see it as fun, when she hadn't been the one facing a cold dose of reality.

"And you stopped dating." Angela wasn't letting this go, her eyes locked onto Abby. "Until you got together with Sam, and you begged me. *Begged* me. Not to tell him all the shit you'd gotten up to. It was, 'Please, Angela, I've started over,' 'Please, Angela, let me reinvent myself.' And I kept quiet. I didn't give anything away. And you locked away all the partying, and all the raunchy shit from college, and you've kept it locked away. You let it out a little bit when you get drunk, and when you're hanging out with me, but with Sam, you're totally buttoned up." She stood back up to her full height. "Ten years is a long time to be buttoned up."

Defensiveness rose inside Abby. "There's nothing wrong with growing up."

"Getting your grades right, paying off your debt, sure. But your sex life? What you want? That's not about growing up. That's squashing who you really are to try to please somebody who'd be happy with you no matter what." Angela put a hand on Abby's shoulder and gave her a gentle shove. "Let out Abby Wood If She Could. See where it goes."

The risk, though. It was easy for Angela to talk about this, when it wasn't her marriage stability hanging in the balance. Old Abby was embarrassing, and she'd been content to keep her irresponsible youth in the past, even if that meant quashing a few of her sexual desires in the process.

Angela waved her hand. "Just think about it. This could lead to a better marriage. A better sex life. To take things up from once a month missionary, or whatever it is you're doing now."

"Hey! Uncalled for." Abby hoisted an entire humidifier off the bottom shelf, ready to dump it in Angela's cart.

Angela wheeled the cart away quickly, laughing. "Stop it, you bitch! Put that back. I'm sorry I insulted you."

Abby put the humidifier back. "Don't get personal." She dusted her hands off on her jeans. "So, what, you think I should just unload all my fantasies on him? I might as well hit him with a two-by-four."

Angela nodded to the end of the aisle. "You could get one of those here."

"Seriously."

"Okay, seriously. You could wait for him to bring it up. Kind of a chicken move, but whatever." Angela shrugged.

"I am going to stuff another humidifier in your cart if you don't quit making fun of me."

Angela grinned. "Fair. So, whatever, you play it by ear. If you're really fine with the way things are, and Sam doesn't bring up anything about the reunion, then you'll know it was a fluke. And if he *does* bring it up, well, take him up on it."

"Maybe." There wasn't much to lose, letting Sam take the lead. Even if it did feel a bit cowardly. College Abby never would have taken the backseat like that. But College Abby made a lot of bad decisions in her time, so she wasn't exactly a reliable inspiration.

Angela turned the corner to another aisle and stopped in front of a whole section of ropes and chains. "Or instead, you could just take him here."

Abby followed her gesture to the display and started to laugh. "That's subtle."

"You never know, right? Everybody's trying this stuff now. One book series goes wild and suddenly it's wall-to-wall handcuffs and leather. Maybe a sexy shopping trip."

"To the Home Depot. Very seductive." Abby picked up

a length of chain, absent-mindedly letting the metal links slip through her fingers. Of all her kinks, bondage was one of the tamer ones, and she couldn't imagine Sam tying her to anything. She shouldn't hope for things to be otherwise, since that way led only to disappointment. Sam was good for her. She'd wanted to change, and once she'd done so, she'd been able to secure a relationship with the best man she'd ever met. She'd made that choice willingly, and if she had it to do over, she'd do everything the same.

"You got everything on your list?" Abby pointed to the notebook in Angela's hand.

Angela put her notebook in her pocket. "I've got it all. Let's check out."

. . .

Ever since the party, Sam couldn't look at Abby without a whole host of inappropriate thoughts. She was beautiful, and he'd always thought she was beautiful, always been attracted to her, but this was...different. He found himself getting distracted by the curve of her ass when she bent over, suddenly picturing her bent over the bed while he slid into her from behind. When she leaned her head back on the couch, he remembered the way she leaned her head back on his collarbone at the reunion, gasping as he rubbed her to orgasm. The most innocuous actions were leaving him stopped in his tracks all week, and it was pretty damn difficult to focus on anything else.

Usually, he didn't bother her for sex during the week. They both had busy schedules, both balanced work and hobbies with their relationship. It was only respectful to give her time to sleep rather than interrupt that with sex. On the weekends, he would move in for kisses that lingered, deepened, intensified into passion, and then they would take their time together until both were satisfied.

Was she bored with him?

She'd clearly had an adventurous past. He'd always thought they were happy, but maybe she had been hiding some kind of deep dissatisfaction. Their sex life now certainly wasn't what she'd been used to. Maybe she wanted more and had just never asked? He'd never thought to offer.

Tonight, though? Sitting next to Abby while they both read in bed, outwardly placid in their evening routine, his whole body twitched with pent-up energy. She'd been a different woman at the reunion, untamed and uninhibited, and he could *not* stop running that evening over and over through his head. Even her stories turned him on. Maybe, just maybe, with the right opportunity, she would indulge that side of herself again.

After setting his book aside, Sam slid over next to Abby. She raised an eyebrow at him. "Can I help you?"

"Want to put that away?"

Abby set her book on the nightstand, and Sam slid over to kiss her. In his arms, she was soft and pliant, going easily into his embrace. She wasn't kissing him like she had at the reunion, untamed and raw. These were the sweet, tender kisses they usually exchanged. He experimented, tilting his head, kissing her harder. She made a soft, surprised noise and kissed back, tangling her fingers in his hair.

He mouthed down her neck, to the juncture of her shoulder, nipping the flesh and making her giggle. She was ticklish there. She let him pull at her plain nightgown, lifting it off and tossing it aside so she lay bare beneath him.

"No underwear again?" he asked. She hadn't worn any to the reunion, either.

Abby shook her head. "I never wear it to sleep. I thought you knew that."

"Seems there's a lot I don't know." He kissed the freckles

dusting her chest, tiny spots of light brown speckling her skin. "You didn't wear panties to the party."

She chuckled, her breasts lifting with the movement. He buried his face in between them, and she sighed sweetly. "Mmm. It's…stockings and garter belts," she answered, one hand drifting up to cup the back of his head. "Panties just get in the way."

"It was so sexy." Sam suckcd one nipple into his mouth, and she arched up against him, letting out a breathy sigh that went straight to his groin. Her nipples were perfect, light pink, barely darker than her skin, large and sensitive. He was always so careful with them, knowing how just the lightest amount of suction made her shiver and moan. At the reunion, though, she'd responded to a much firmer touch. He sank his teeth into the flesh, biting, pressing harder than he'd ever dared. She gasped, hips twitching, and he went from half hard to completely hard in his boxers. He pulled back and smiled. "Tell me about one of the places you fooled around on campus."

Abby laughed breathlessly as he returned to her nipple. "Nah. It's in the past."

He switched sides, laving attention on the other nipple, teasing and then biting the same way, rewarded by her gasp. "I want to hear about it."

Her breath came ragged as he kept up the rough contact, biting and sucking, each twitch a signal to continue. "It was a long time ago," she said, gasping. "You tell me. Tell me something…from your past."

"I don't have anything exciting in my past. You know that." He kissed her stomach, the soft curve of her belly where it dimpled in around her waist. "Nothing public. Nothing interesting. Not like you."

Abby scooted up to sitting, pushing him gently away. "Wait a minute. Wait. Are you just trying to get me to tell you dirty stories? Because I can talk dirty if you want to."

"No, not that." He didn't need her fictionalized stories of what she thought he wanted to hear. "I want to hear about you."

Abby frowned. Sam leaned in to kiss the frown, teasing her lips with his. She made a soft noise of interest, then one of annoyance, and pulled away. "I don't understand. Why do you want to hear about me?"

He might as well be a little more direct. "I think it's hot. It turns me on. I thought it would be sexy to have you tell me about some things from your past. Like what you did back when you were in college."

Abby laughed, the light laugh when she wasn't taking something seriously. "I'd rather not."

"Why not? Don't you trust me?" He sat up the rest of the way. "We're married, Abby. I'm committed to you. Forever. Remember this?" He pointed to the band around his finger. "I'm not gonna just go walk out on you because you, what, blew some guy in the library stacks?"

"So what if I did blow some guy in the library stacks?" She pulled the covers up over her naked body, leaning back against the headboard. "And I did, by the way. But it's not really your business."

"No, I know." Shoot. She was getting mad, and he didn't want to make her mad. "I like it. I like seeing this part of you. I want to get to know this side of you better."

Abby shook her head. "You aren't that kind of guy."

So this was about him. The pang of disappointment closed his throat for a moment. Maybe he could prove her wrong. "Try me."

Abby sighed. She looked off toward the wall, arms folded over the sheet. "I don't know. That side of me…doesn't exist anymore. To bring it all back, it's like…we're better off just not going there. Opening a can of worms. You can't unknow

something, and I don't want you to think any less of me."
She turned back to him. "Especially when you aren't sharing
anything of yours."

They were back to that again. "I've told you literally
everything in my past, even if not in detail. I dated some
women. Some short-term relationships, some longer
relationships. We had pretty straightforward sex. Nothing
exciting, nothing public, nothing experimental. Nothing
kinky."

"See, there. What do you even think is kinky?" She let
the sheets slip, one rose-colored nipple peeking over the edge.
His gaze was drawn to it. The hard tip was barely concealed
by the sheet, just begging for his fingers, his mouth. He had to
look away, back up to her face.

"What we did the other night at the reunion. That was
kinky."

Abby blushed. He loved her blushes, the way her skin
turned rosy, her complexion mottling out the freckles. She
blushed not just on her face, but on her shoulders and neck as
well, her whole body giving away when she was embarrassed…
or aroused. "Okay. That was kinky. But that wasn't like you. I
don't want to go unloading a whole bunch from my past and
have you, like, never want to sleep with me again. Just so you
can temporarily get your rocks off thinking about a fantasy
that, in reality, I doubt you'd actually want to do."

A fantasy he wouldn't want to do? He'd do anything if
it meant she would share her honest self with him. "At the
reunion, that was hot. That was some of the hottest fun we've
had together, and it wasn't even *sex* sex. I want to spice things
up with you like that."

Abby continued to look at him, uncertain, so he pressed
on. "Don't you want to spice things up with me?"

Abby fidgeted with the edge of the sheet. "I don't mind
the way things are now," she said, but her voice was flat, the

tone she got when she was lying.

He might as well call her on it. "Bullshit."

Her nostrils flared. "Okay, fine. It hasn't been really exciting, no, but I don't have a *problem* with it. People don't just fuck like they're newlyweds forever."

It hadn't even been that different when they were newlyweds, with Sam always trying to show Abby he respected her and would take good care of her. He waited, and the silence between them stretched out while she looked thoughtful and more than a little apprehensive. Finally, she looked back over at him. "But if you want to spice things up, I'm not opposed to it."

Not opposed. That was a start. *Not opposed* was a far cry from how soaking wet she'd been when he'd fingered her on the porch at the reunion. But if she didn't want to admit to it, he didn't need to push. "How about if we forget the past entirely, and try this from another angle?"

She furrowed her brow, cautious. "Like what?"

The idea was slowly spinning itself up in his mind. "How about instead of you telling me about your past, we focus on the present? We could play a game."

Abby pursed her lips. "What kind of game?"

"We each take turns sharing a sexual fantasy. Something we'd really like to try. And if the other person is interested, too, we make them come true."

Abby tipped her head to the side. She relaxed her arms, so the blanket slipped down more, all the way off her breasts. "Are you just going to try to one-up me? Try to prove that you're kinky?"

"I might be kinky. I don't know." He wouldn't know unless he tried, right? Was that something people automatically knew about themselves? He needed her to at least try this, to let him show himself as more than whatever boring stick-in-the-mud she must consider him to be. "But I know that I'm interested in spicing things up with you, and this is one way to do that."

"What if one of us comes up with something the other one doesn't want to do?" she asked.

"We don't do it." That seemed obvious. "The game ends whenever we want it to. There's no winner or loser or anything." Even saying it, though, he knew that was only a half-truth. He would be game for whatever she threw at him, no matter what. She might try to call his bluff, but he wasn't bluffing. There might not be a winner or loser, officially, but he was going to win. She would see that she hadn't made a mistake choosing him. He could be as adventurous as she wanted.

"All right." She nodded. "You're on."

• • •

For a few moments, they looked at each other. He was going to look away first, for sure, and Abby kept a hard stare on Sam. This game was...interesting. Definitely out of character for him. She almost felt bad for him. She could unload the big guns right away, pull out one of her really fucked-up fantasies and get him to call everything off, but she didn't want to totally freak him out. Maybe she'd lob him some kind of softball, some fantasy that pushed the envelope a little.

Before she could come up with anything, though, he said, "I'll start."

"Oh?" Another surprise. Something uneasy settled in her stomach. Maybe he had a secret side, too, like she did. Was that even possible? How much did she not know about Sam? But no. He was a pretty easy-to-read guy. Transparent, direct, these were qualities she valued in him from the day they'd met. After college, she'd had enough of games for a lifetime. How ironic that now they were turning back to another one.

"Yeah. I have to think about it first, though." He grinned at her and stripped off his shirt. Damn, that line of muscles was always enough to distract her from anything she was doing at the moment. He went to CrossFit so often, his body was built lean and strong. He was hard where she was soft, every inch of him a complement to her plump curves.

It wasn't just his body, though. She was definitely turned on at the idea of this game. "So you don't have a fantasy just ready to lay on me?"

"Nope." He moved closer, crawling on his hands and knees until he was face-to-face with her. This room had suddenly grown much hotter.

"You think I'm just going to fuck you now?" she teased.

"Yeah. I do." He tipped his head to the side. "Because I think the idea of this game has you as hot as I am." With his eyes locked on hers, he inched the sheet down, baring the rest of her body, and carefully dipped his fingers into the folds between her legs.

Abby's eyelids fluttered, mouth falling open in a sigh. Little ripples of pleasure floated up her spine. He never went right at her like this; he always built up to it with kisses and more gentle touches. This was foreign, bold, and she was soaking wet.

"You like this," he said, voice tinged with wonder.

"Mm-hmm." She smiled in acquiescence, scooting down the bed to lie on her back. His fingers were dancing over her clit enough to muddle her brain.

"You think you've got me figured out, don't you?"

Abby opened her eyes at his question. Sam lay beside her, propped up on one elbow, his expression curious. She didn't answer, instead tucking an arm behind her head. She lifted one leg, bending it at the knee, giving him more access to her clit. "I don't know. Maybe you'll surprise me."

He quirked an eyebrow. Lost in those eyes, she gasped at

a sudden feeling of fullness making her muscles twitch. His fingers slid deep inside her, more than usual, probably three, wide and thick and definitely more than she was expecting. "Fuck," she gasped, catching her breath. "Yeah, that's a surprise." Her light chuckle made her clench around his fingers, taking her breath away once more.

"Tell me what you like." Sam's fingers shifted, curling, pressing up against her G-spot, making her see stars again. "Pretend this is the first time."

So he was going to make her talk. This wasn't what they normally did; if they talked during sex, it was playful or joking, fun instead of intense. His expression was deadly serious, though, his eyes dark with arousal.

"Well, I like that." She tried to laugh, but pressure on her clit turned that laugh into a moan. The heel of his hand pressed against her, rubbing just like he had when he'd fingered her on the deck.

"Tell me," he repeated. "Do you like the full feeling?"

She nodded, for a moment the words caught in her throat. "Yes. Stretched...oh." He was fucking her harder with his hand. "Not so fast. Slow." He slowed down, pressing and pulling back, circling her clit with his palm. "I want your cock."

"No. Not yet."

Abby's eyes opened; when had she closed them? He was serious; he wasn't going to fuck her yet. Fine, he wanted her to ask for things? She would. "My nipples. I like...when you suck on them."

He bent his head to obey. That was nice, sweet, the tight pull of his mouth, but not enough. Before she could ask for more, though, he bit down, just like he had at the start of tonight, harder and rougher than usual. The pain sparked like a bright light behind her eyes. That was so good, and she arched up against his hand. He didn't need to be told to switch sides, his mouth rough on her other nipple as well, sucking to the point of pain before closing his teeth on that nub. She clenched around his fingers, his hand making obscene wet noises between her legs.

It wasn't fair that she be the only one to enjoy this. She pushed him away, shoving him over onto his back, his fingers sliding from her body. Before he could ask, she held up a finger. "It's my turn." But then, just because she could, just because he wouldn't expect it, she took his fingers into her mouth and sucked her juices off them.

"Fucking hell." His head slammed back against the pillow.

"I like the way I taste."

His eyes went wide like he'd seen nirvana, and shit, she could blow his mind with almost no effort at all. Because yeah, she *did* like the way she tasted, even though maybe that was weird, and she liked the way he tasted, too. She tugged his boxers off—how was he still wearing them?—and sucked the head of his cock into her mouth.

"Ah, fuck," he swore. He didn't swear as much as she did, only in moments like this, when he was overwhelmed.

Abby lapped the slit and looked at him. "Tell me what *you* like."

Sam had gone completely inarticulate in the time it took her to put her mouth on him, but he managed to stammer out some words. "That. I like that."

"Yeah? You like when I suck your dick?" She slid her mouth over him again. His heavy weight against her tongue, the sensation of her mouth being filled, she loved the whole experience of giving a blow job. They didn't do this that much. Not nearly often enough for how pleasurable it was, that sense of control…but no, more than that. He could take control at any time as well, grab her hair and force her mouth down onto him. Not that Sam would ever do such a thing, though, unless maybe she really persuaded him into it.

"I like your tongue. And when you take me so deep…" His words trailed off as she did that, relaxing her throat, letting him push past her gag reflex so she could swallow him down. His voice jumped a half octave. "Damn, Abby." He touched her head, which wasn't a surprise, since he often brushed her hair back in moments like this.

He wanted to know what she liked? Fine. She licked her way off him. "Pull my hair."

He paused only a moment, hesitation present in the frozen way his fingers touched her, and then he slid his palm through her hair and closed his hand into a fist. Shit, that was *perfect,* needles of pain rippling across her scalp, pulling out a whimper from between her lips. When she bent to take him into her mouth again, this time, he used his grip on her hair to push her down even more.

She relaxed her throat and moaned, just absolutely *moaned* around his dick, and he began to use his grip to hold her in place and thrust. Maybe this was instinct, something any guy would do if given the chance, but it wasn't any guy. It was Sam, Sam the straitlaced architect, who was professional and courteous and who'd never done anything wild. Sam was pulling her hair and fucking her mouth like never before, and Abby had a hand between her legs rubbing her clit before she was fully conscious of what she was doing.

"You're so good at this, babe." He relaxed his grip on her hair, and she came up for air, gasping, licking her swollen lips. She wanted him right now, this need surging up inside her more than just lust. She wanted to claim, to own, to possess.

Instead, he moved first, rolling her onto her back, slotting himself between her thighs like he had hundreds of times before.

"Bend my knee back," she directed.

Sam lifted one of her legs up to press against her chest,

opening her up even more to him. His grip tightened on her calf as he slid into her soaked pussy.

No matter how many times they did this, the first thrust took her breath away. A strangled groan escaped her at the overwhelming sensation of being split open on his cock. This position was a whole different level. He was able to reach deeper, penetrating farther, rubbing against some spots deep, deep inside her pussy he'd never hit before. This wasn't her G-spot, it was something else, something that had her moaning.

Normally, Sam's thrusts were measured, controlled, deep and slow enough that she could take the time she needed to reach orgasm. Tonight, he was different. Tonight, he fucked her hard, using that grip on her leg to slam into her.

"Just like that," she said, voice tight, the thrust lighting her up from the inside. "Hard. It's so good." She swore, the curses spilling out of her, something tightening deep in her groin.

"Yeah. Perfect," he groaned. "Just…take it."

Take it? He was never rough with her, and this wasn't an act. His eyes locked onto hers, fierce, focused, jaw tight, his thrusts erratic and blunt. He was like a different person entirely, like Sam but some other variant of him, and Abby couldn't look away from those deep eyes. She wasn't even touching her clit, her hands gripping his arms instead, and each thrust rubbed perfectly so she was spiraling up before she expected.

Sometimes her climaxes took a while, eyes closed and lips tight, focused on the sensations without the distraction of thinking of anything else. Not tonight. Just like the reunion, she was on the edge quickly, overwhelmed, her climax tightening inside her like a dam that would burst at any moment. Each muscle clenched, body poised to leap from that precipice.

The pleasure split open all at once, orgasm exploding outward from her core, nerves firing as she clenched and clenched and clenched around the cock inside her. She was lost, toes curling in the sheets, as Sam buried himself all the way deep and came hot and wet inside her. Boneless, she collapsed, her leg slipping down and to the side as Sam's arms gave way and he lay down on her.

They breathed, quiet and overwhelmed, into the silence between them. Abby blinked her eyes open at last, catching her breath, the weight of Sam's body a solid presence on hers.

Maybe she'd been wrong. Maybe there was more to Sam than she'd ever thought.

Maybe *she* was the one who needed to be afraid of what they'd begun.

Chapter Three

The Night Owl was arguably the best bar in town for the drinks alone, never mind the nostalgia. Every time Sam walked in the place, it felt like home. He had years' worth of memories there: back when he and Abby were dating, they used to grab a nightcap at the Night Owl after seeing a show, cozied up in one of the booths in the back where nobody bothered them. But now, it was the bastion of guy time, the favorite hangout for his CrossFit buddies after another grueling workout. He was last to arrive, the others already gathered around their usual round table in the front window, holding beers and mixed drinks.

They were an odd group: on the far side of the table sat Mitchell, the person Sam had met first when he joined CrossFit. Built solid and broad like a refrigerator, Mitchell, with his blond hair and crystal blue eyes, he had a sort of "European warrior" look. Next to him, Deshawn sat in stark contrast, short and lean, a light-skinned Black man with thin dreadlocks tied back. Deshawn was the scrappy sort of workout partner, the kind who could outlast almost anybody and was competitive enough to try to really do it. Rounding out the trio was Jack, average build, average height, a white guy with short, spiky brown hair and glasses. He'd joined their group most recently, a student at the university using CrossFit to unwind from the stress of his PhD program. They all looked up as Sam slid into the empty chair and joined them.

"Geez, did I take that long? You've all got drinks already." Sam looked around for their server, who was nowhere to be seen.

"You take the longest showers." Mitchell shook his head. "I managed to shower and get over here before you, and I walked." He managed a cross between soft-spoken and no-nonsense, probably useful when he was running the kitchen at the Mapleton Pub. Out of everybody in this group, Mitchell was probably the one Sam felt closest to, but they didn't really hang out outside of these guys' nights and the gym.

"Walking's easier, though," Sam protested. "Parking's a bitch."

Deshawn, shaking his head, lifted up a glass in a toast. "Here's to that, man. I'm in the garage."

"The garage is a pussy move." Jack shook his head. "Real men parallel park."

Deshawn raised his eyebrows. "Dude, I saw you park, and you are like three and a half feet from that curb. Don't give me shit about the garage when you're out here parking like my half-blind grandma."

Sam laughed, along with the rest of them, even Jack. He looked over the menu. "Mitchell, what's good on tap right now?" There were perks to having friends who owned a brew pub.

"They've got one of our seasonal ones, and they also have an IPA that Ben's been really into." Mitchell raised his rocks glass. "I have had it up to here with beer right now, so I am drinking whisky."

Sam ordered the seasonal beer, and conversation shifted to the holidays and what they'd done since they last grabbed a beer together, well before Christmas.

"You spent New Year's at Abby's college reunion?" Deshawn shook his head. "Reunions are horrible. Do you know how much shit my classmates give me about being a nurse?"

"Your classmates are assholes," Mitchell responded before turning back to Sam. "How was the reunion?"

"It was actually pretty fun. I got to meet some of her old college friends." Sam hadn't minded at all, even without the kinky shit at the end. That wasn't something he was going to bring up here, though.

"You mean her college boyfriends?" Jack grinned, drinking his beer.

Sam had gotten his beer by then, so he knocked his glass gently against Jack's like it was a toast. "We've been married almost seven years, guys. It's not like her past makes much of a difference anymore."

Fat likelihood that was true, but these guys didn't need to know the difference. Sam raised his chin to Mitchell. "What about you? You do anything fun over the holidays?"

Mitchell smiled the small, tight-lipped smile he often gave that seemed as though he had more going on than he let on. He was an enigmatic guy, a tough nut to crack, as it were. "Visited some family before the holiday, and then we stayed local. Ben made me close the restaurant on Christmas and New Year's Day, so I actually had some rest."

Ben. Ben ran the restaurant with Mitchell, shouldering the brewing half of their operation. His relationship with Mitchell, though, was a lot less clear. Sam had always just assumed they were partners, because they spent so much time together, but maybe they weren't. It was difficult to know with Mitchell, and if he wasn't telling, Sam wasn't in a place to ask.

Even if he was curious from time to time.

By the time they got back to Jack, he was halfway done with his drink and had this mischievous, shit-eating grin on his face. "Listen. I know we don't normally talk about this shit. But I have to tell you what Collette and I did over New Year's."

Deshawn put his glass down. "I know that look. It's something freaky, isn't it?"

Sam couldn't help his own curiosity. Deshawn was right; they weren't the type of guys to dish locker room talk at the bar, except maybe some innuendo and harmless jokes. Jack looked like he was gonna explode, though, actually vibrating with excitement.

Jack didn't wait any longer for them to guess. "We went to a sex club!" he shouted. Realizing his volume, he ducked his head and repeated it, more quietly. "We went to a sex club."

Mitchell put down his whisky. "Where is there a sex club in Mapleton?"

"Not in Mapleton. In Boston. There's this club, and it's invite only. Really high-class. But Collette, she knows the owners through her last roommate. And she got us an invitation."

Sam shifted on his barstool. A sex club in Boston? He'd never been to one of those, never even knew what went on at one. Was that legal? So many questions started bubbling up, but the thought of asking them was embarrassing.

Thoughts of Abby flashed into his mind, of her insinuating that he wasn't the type of person to push his boundaries. Well, he could *be* that kind of person. He just had to tap into that part of himself. "I don't know what happens at a sex club," he managed to ask out loud. "Is it just group sex?"

"Nah, not really." Jack looked around again, but nobody

was listening to them. "I mean, there's some of that. The top floor is the 'dungeon'"—he put it in air quotes—"where all the kinky shit goes on. The other floors are a little of everything. Some of it's really chill, like a normal club, people out having a drink and chatting, but people fool around right there in the open. There're rooms with two-way mirrors, and glory holes, and all the stuff that I seriously never thought existed outside of porn." He shook his head. "Toys, sex swings, kinky stuff, you name it."

"Was it weird?" Deshawn asked. "Seeing people fucking all around you?"

"Not as weird as I'd thought," Jack said. "Mostly I had to get used to all the dicks."

"Were you nervous?" Sam asked. He'd be nervous, obviously, but Jack probably wouldn't admit it.

To his surprise, Jack laughed and nodded. "Hell yes. I almost chickened out, but I thought, what are my chances of ever getting to do something like this again? So I said yes."

"So this was her idea, not yours?" Deshawn asked.

"Hers, definitely. No way I would have thought to ask her to do something like that. But she's kind of a freak, and said it was always on her bucket list, so hell, why not?" Jack looked just delighted with himself, and his enthusiasm was contagious.

"You think you'll go back?" Sam asked.

"I don't know. Maybe. It's a cool thing to do once, but I'm not sure if it's really for me long-term." Jack rubbed the back of his neck, ducking his head nervously. "I'm not an exhibitionist kind of guy, and Collette just wanted to try it once, I think. I don't think it was something she'd want to do again, either."

Out of the group, only Mitchell had been silent, thoughtfully contemplating the whole conversation. Deshawn nudged him. "Nothing to say over there, Mr. Silent?"

Mitchell smiled. "I was just wondering if it's something I might want to try in the future."

Well damn, that made Sam look at Mitchell again. The guy was so full of secrets, never letting out anything about his relationship.

"If you're interested, let me know," Jack said. "Collette can get in touch with you. Her friend said any friend of ours is a friend of hers, or something like that. Anyway, invite's open."

The idea was fully formed in Sam's mind before he'd consciously thought about it, and he turned back to his beer with a new plan.

By the time he got home that night, after finishing his beer and conversation with the guys, Abby was in the shower. Pottery was a messy endeavor, and on studio nights, she liked to take a long, hot shower to relax and clean up. He opened the door to the bathroom, steam rushing out past him and dissolving in the cooler air of the bedroom as he stepped inside.

"That you?" Abby asked from behind the curtain.

Sam smiled. "Nope. I'm a masked stranger, here to ravish you."

Abby peeked out at him. Her red hair was pulled up in a messy bun on top of her head to keep it dry, and without her makeup, she looked like she could be college-age again. She gave him a smile. "I don't know. I'm so tired from all those other masked strangers, I might not have energy to service another one." She ducked back behind the shower curtain.

"Bummer. I'll just have to take my first fantasy elsewhere, then."

Abby reemerged from behind the curtain, pulling it back enough that he could see the curve of one breast. "Your fantasy is a masked stranger fantasy?"

"No. I've got something else." He didn't want to pitch it

like this, though. "I'll wait until you get out."

Abby pursed her lips, eyes narrowing in suspicion. "Okay. I'll hurry up."

"Take your time." Sam waved her off and returned to the living room.

She came out in record time, wearing pajama pants and a loose tank top, her hair now down from its bun. "All right," she said before she'd even come all the way into the room. "Let's hear it. Your first fantasy." She sat next to him on the couch, one leg folded up beneath her.

He'd been rehearsing different ways to ask or say this, but direct seemed best. "There's a sex club in Boston, and I want you to go with me."

Abby blinked. "A sex club?" She tipped her head to the side, uncertainty in her expression. "Like where people go and watch other people fuck? You know a place like that?"

"Yes. Exactly like that." He had already messaged Collette by way of Jack before driving home. "I know about one, and I can get us onto the guest list."

Abby was sitting upright, her body posture tense, and studied Sam like she just didn't know what to make of him. "Do you want to fuck other people?"

"What? No!" Where did she get that idea? "I want to watch other people with you. Maybe do a bit of fooling around of our own, if you're up for that. Whatever you're comfortable with."

Abby looked hesitant, and he hadn't expected that.

"You don't have to say yes," he said quickly. "If you're not comfortable, we can call this whole thing off. Or I can share a different fantasy."

Abby shook her head. "No. I'm game."

"You ever been to a sex club before?"

She gave a short laugh. "Definitely not."

"All right." He pulled out his phone. "How's next

weekend?"

. . .

This definitely wasn't what Abby had pictured when Sam had mentioned sex club. This wasn't a nightclub, or a seedy-looking building with a bouncer out front, and there were no bright neon signs or anything to give away the purpose at all. But the address on Sam's phone matched this nondescript brownstone building in front of them, right on the outskirts of Cambridge, not far from fucking Harvard itself.

"This looks like somebody's house." She glanced around at all the other businesses on the block. "You sure we're at the right place?"

"Collette said we wouldn't recognize it from the outside." Sam put his phone in his pocket and took her hand. "Come on. Let's go check it out."

Abby pulled her long coat more tightly around her and walked with him up the stairs. All week, she'd been waiting for the proverbial other shoe to drop. The Sam she knew would never have suggested they go to a sex club. She hadn't even been sure he knew sex clubs actually existed; hell, she'd kind of thought they were legendary as well. Three possibilities existed: either he was into all these things and had been hiding his true self from her, he wasn't into any of it but doing it to prove something to himself or to her, or maybe he wasn't sure and was open to trying it out. The first option was unsettling, because it would mean she didn't know him at all. The second option was frustrating, because it meant he was doing stuff he didn't like for a stupid reason. The third option, though, was the most intriguing. If he was at least somewhat interested in what they were doing, then maybe Angela was right, and they had some "spice up" potential. Any minute, though, he was probably going to turn around and tell her he wasn't up for this.

A short, plump young woman waited right inside the front door, at a sort of hostess stand. She looked like she should be selling them a mortgage, all chipper attitude and business attire, with wide, friendly eyes that didn't fit Abby's mental image of "person who takes names at a sex club."

The host scanned through a list of names on her tablet and found them. "It says here you're first-timers." She smiled and set her tablet down. "Welcome. I'll go over the ground rules with you before you go in, and they're posted in several places in case you forget. First, watching is encouraged, but no touching unless you're invited to do so. Any form of verbal or physical harassment will result in being removed from the club. We recommend fluid barriers and provide them in each room. Please clean up after yourselves. If you would like a break, this first room you're going to enter is a designated sex-free lounge. Street-legal dress is required in the lounge, but other than that, beyond this door, clothing choices are up to you. The dungeon on the third floor has its own set of rules posted outside, so please familiarize yourself with those if you'd like to make use of that space. Do you have any questions?"

Abby and Sam looked at each other and shrugged. That all seemed to be pretty much common sense.

"All right, then, here's a map of the space." She handed them a photocopied map of the building layout, which someone had labeled by hand to indicate all the various rooms. She tapped a spot on the map. "Right past the lounge are changing rooms and places to store your things if you need them." She flashed them a bright smile. "Have fun tonight!"

The lounge just past the door was dimly lit, especially after the brightness of the foyer, and Abby stopped short as her eyes adjusted. The music was fairly quiet, too, soft jazz that blended with low sounds of conversation. A few couples were chatting quietly, wrapped in robes or wearing street clothes, one pair just cuddled together on a loveseat. They hung up their coats in the coat closet. Abby had gone with a little black dress for the night, simple and classy, but she'd second-guessed the decision a few times, considering fancy lingerie or something a bit slinkier than this simple cocktail dress. Now, she was happy to be wearing a full outfit. Already, her heart beat in her throat, tight with anticipation and uncertainty. She'd never done anything like this before, and Sam had been pretty vague about his interest.

His hand on the small of her back grounded her. "You ready to go on? Or you want to stay in here for a while?"

At the other end of the room, two changing room doors flanked a central door leading to, presumably, the rest of the club.

"I didn't come to a sex club to stay in the lounge." Hopefully she sounded braver than she felt as she took his hand. "Come on."

Past that door, a pulsing bass beat drowned out the smooth jazz from the lounge. *Here* was the sight Abby had been expecting. One wall was resplendent with a full bar lit in blue, where a bartender mixed drinks for two completely naked women chatting with him. One section of the room was a dance floor, complete with poles, although no one was dancing. On the other side of the room, couches and love seats hosted numerous couples and small groups, mostly half or completely naked, all engrossed in their partners.

Abby stopped short. The woman at the front had said that watching was encouraged, but no one there was watching. Everyone was…participating. This didn't feel as sexy as it had at the reunion, when they'd been hiding and trying not to get caught. Her stomach fluttered with a wave of uncertainty, and Sam touched her back once more, just as he had done in the other room.

"You want to get a drink?" he asked.

The bartender greeted them with a warm smile and a nod. He was a handsome guy rocking a full beard and the hipster look, complete with suspenders and bow tie. "First time?" he said loud enough to be heard over the music.

"Is it that obvious?" Abby climbed onto one of the stools near the naked women, who were still there in conversation with each other. Sam sat beside her.

"A little." The bartender smiled. "But don't worry. It's everybody's first time at some point." He extended a hand. "I'm Bill. I own the place."

They introduced themselves as Abby's jitters settled into a low background hum instead of intense quaking. They ordered drinks, and finally, Abby let herself look around in more detail. She couldn't hear much over the music, and maybe that was the point. People could lose themselves in here, in the patterned lights and the throbbing bass line.

Bill passed them their drinks across the counter. "You know, if you want something a bit less noisy, keep heading down the hall. The next room might be more your speed. Feel free to take your drinks."

Sam paid and tipped, sliding close enough to put an arm around Abby's waist. "Let's go check it out," he said.

As soon as the door closed behind them, leaving them in a short hallway, the music sounds faded down to just the pulsing bass. This hallway had two doors on each side, each bearing a sign. The first door on both sides was labeled "to be watched," and the second, "to watch." At the end of the hallway, a single unlabeled door led into the room beyond, and that's where Abby headed.

The quiet sounds of sex hit her ears before anything else. Something about that noise thrummed a chord inside her, lighting fireworks along her nerves even with no one touching her. This room was as large as the previous one, lit by dim lights and candles, with two king-sized beds and a handful of couches. Caught up in the events happening in front of her, Abby edged over to an empty couch and sat. She took one sip of her drink and set it aside, drawn instead to this scene.

On the bed closest to her, a woman lay stretched out, naked, her long brown hair loose across the pillow. A man lay alongside her, his mouth on her breast, his other hand gently tweaking her other nipple, completely focused on her body. They weren't alone, though; another man knelt between her legs, holding her thighs apart, working her over with his mouth.

Sam sank down beside Abby, also staring at the scene in front of them. Their couch faced the side of the bed, where they could see everything. The woman had her head turned toward them, eyes closed but lips parted, and in the quiet of the room, each of her breaths was audible. Abby was breathing in rhythm with her before she realized it, shallow, soft breaths, like she was the one being pleasured. The man between her legs was taking his time, wet noises intimate and nearly obscene.

Sam's body pressed warm against Abby's side, turning toward her, one hand moving to her thigh and burning her skin through the fabric of her dress. "You like watching?" he murmured, so low no one else could hear. "Like the other night on the porch?"

Abby nodded, not wanting to make a sound and disturb everything. She was wet. She pressed her legs more tightly together, a tiny shiver of intensity racing through her groin.

Sam draped an arm over her shoulder and began to idly brush his fingertips across her breast. Her nipple poked against the fabric of the dress, and his touch barely registered, tiny ticklish brushes sending shivers all through her body. She was already sensitive, and his too-light touch was making her even *more* sensitive. Maybe he knew. Pressed against her like this, he could probably feel her response, the way her breath quickened, nipple tightening into a sharp peak. And still, gentle, endlessly gentle brushes.

His other hand inched below the hemline of her cocktail dress, then began to skim lightly upward.

Abby's breath caught as Sam brushed the juncture of her thighs. She wasn't wearing underwear, Sam's only directive for tonight, and when he coaxed her legs apart, the air brushed cold over her superheated skin. She turned to speak, but he chose that moment to twist her nipple through her dress and swallow her sharp gasp of pain.

"Shh," he whispered against her lips. "Watch."

The woman on the bed gasped louder, drawing Abby's gaze, and Sam slipped his fingers up between her folds to find her clit. Two fingers pressed against it, hard, and a jolt like lightning sizzled all the way up through her body. Abby gasped, shock and surprise and arousal all in one. The woman in front of her gripped the sheets beneath her, her pale skin flushing pink, tossing her head from side to side as her expression wavered between pleasure and pain. The man who had been sucking her breasts was whispering to her now, his hands still teasing her skin, murmuring something no one but them could hear.

"She's going to come." Sam's voice came so close in her ear. "I wonder if he's reminding her that everyone's watching."

Abby shivered. If it were her on that bed, that's what she'd want, the tantalizing reminder of her own vulnerability and helplessness. Just the thought of it made her pussy throb as Sam's steady, talented fingers worked her over.

Sam nipped her earlobe. "People are watching you, you know."

Abby tried to turn her head to see, but Sam shushed her. "No. Watch the bed. The couple next to us keeps looking over here. And at the foot of the bed, there's a man who's watching you more than he's watching her. Do you like that?"

She whimpered, the noise tumbling out at the mere thought of this. Words wouldn't come, so she nodded. She loved the thought of it, loved it even as it made her blush all the way to her hair, the conflicting embarrassment and arousal potent as a drug. Between her legs, Sam still teased her tender clit, dragging his fingers up and down, lighting every one of her nerves on fire.

On the bed, the woman was starting to shudder, her hips twitching, and the man eating her pussy held her more tightly. Her gasps became moans, broken, needy, desperate, the kind of noises Abby was so close to making herself, noises of overwhelming desire. Abby's clit throbbed with each pass of Sam's fingers. Finally, the woman on the bed arched up, shuddering, her mouth open in a keening cry. Abby moaned, pussy clenching once around nothing, and fuck, she wanted this, wanted to come, wanted this teasing to escalate until she, too, was crying out in pleasure.

The woman writhed away from the man who had his arms locked around her thighs, unable to escape him, twitching from what must be too much sensation. "Please," she sobbed.

Finally, the man released her, and both of them lay on either side of her, kissing her and then each other as she shuddered into silence. Abby's pulse thrummed in her veins, her body still so tense and unfulfilled.

"You want more?" Sam asked into her ear, and she nodded. He smiled and moved his fingers out from between her legs.

She whined, hips chasing his hand from reflex, and he chuckled. "You like it when they're watching you, don't you?"

She hadn't exactly hidden that well, had she?

"How about those rooms in the hallway?"

Abby shifted on the couch to look more directly at Sam. The threesome on the bed still lounged together, resting in the afterglow. Around them, some people were getting up and leaving, others were getting further into their own action. No one was paying her and Sam much attention anymore.

"The rooms in the hallway?" They'd had "to be watched" and "to watch" signs. She could figure out the rest. "You want people to watch us?"

"I was thinking of something else." He seemed hesitant, the first time all night. "I'd really like…to watch you."

Abby swallowed. Could she do that? Be alone in a room while Sam watched her, probably through a peephole or two-way glass? Her body still twitched with pent-up arousal, desire mingling with all those heady hormones in her blood.

"Will you be the only one watching me?" she asked.

"Do you want me to be?"

Of course he would ask. She closed her eyes. Sam had taken her here, had already done more than she'd expected. Maybe she could dip a toe in and admit some of her own exhibitionism. "I…am okay with it either way."

Sam made his own needy, low noise, a growl, and caught her behind the neck to kiss her. His mouth pressed hard against hers, devouring, and heat bloomed all over Abby's skin. There was no way she'd say no to any of this, no matter what he wanted, not when this so clearly turned him on.

He pushed away, like he had to force himself to break the kiss. "Come on."

• • •

Abby stood in front of the bed and stared at the large two-way mirror on the wall. All she could see was herself: long red hair, flushed skin, black cocktail dress hugging her curves. On the other side of that mirror was Sam, and maybe other people. She'd locked this door so no one else could come in. Here, she was alone, and whatever she chose to do, he'd be watching.

He'd be watching, and he might not be alone. She had no way of knowing.

That was the hottest part, honestly; the uncertainty tingled in her blood like the alcohol. Sam could be the only one on the other side of this mirror or he could be part of a crowd, everyone captivated by the sight of her. She might as well put on a show, right?

She reached behind her back to unzip the dress, then carefully, slowly, peeled it off her body. With each inch, she revealed herself to the mirror and the watchers beyond. It pooled on the floor, and she bent to toss it onto a nearby chair. She wore only a lace bra beneath it, no garter belts or stockings tonight, nothing to get in the way. The lace did not conceal anything about her full breasts and hard pink nipples, and she unfastened it to toss aside. Now she was naked, for God and everyone, her own body completely visible in this mirror. Not having to look at her audience was easier; she could imagine whatever she wanted, whether it was someone watching or not.

She imagined someone watching.

Her hands skimmed over her curves, lingering on her breasts, full and sensitive. She gently rolled her nipples between her fingers, eyes falling closed. Her nipples were a direct line to her clit, tiny sparks of pleasure escalating fast even without more contact. Her whole body tingled like a live wire tonight.

She needed more.

Abby lay back on the bed and turned her head to stare at her own reflection in the mirror, one hand skimming down to her already swollen clit. Sam had turned her on so much, and the lightest touch made her gasp. She began to rub faster. She was going to come like this, for Sam and everyone, letting total strangers watch her in this most intimate moment. She'd never done anything like this before. She'd fooled around with boyfriends in public places, sure, mastered the whole Campus Twenty, but she wasn't the one being pleasured, being vulnerable. She wasn't the one being watched. Now, she was the object of their stares. It was enough to make her pussy drip.

If only she had a cock inside her. Reaching her other hand down between her legs, she slid two fingers inside to fuck herself. That felt so good, that width to clench around, not as good as a cock but still enough to make her sigh. Could they hear her? Maybe her sounds were amplified in there, the small room listening to every moan and gasp, every wet, slick sound of her fingers working in and out. She was already on the edge, body teetering toward climax, and she slowed down and forced herself to wait.

This was torturous, this edging, and she never did it with Sam. She let him take her to climax without delay, loving to share that pleasure with him, but sometimes when she was alone, she made herself wait. Just like this, holding off at the edge, lingering until she thought she might scream. Even now, her body yearned for that rush, that release, and she forced her breathing to slow, unclenching her muscles, fighting the gorgeous inevitability. Nothing else made her feel so out of control, so desperate. If Sam were doing this to her, she would do anything for him right now, yield to any of his wishes.

He could ask her to beg.

He could ask her to use a toy, to fuck herself on it for the amusement of her audience.

He could bring in someone else, another man watching her play with herself, and tell her to fuck him. And she would say yes.

She clenched reflexively once, pussy spasming around her fingers at just that thought, and that was it. Her climax slammed into her, doubly strong for having been delayed, and she curled up off the bed with the intensity of the waves. Her whole body tensed as pleasure-pain ripped through her, taking her breath in gasps and cries, leaving her wracked with trembling so fierce she couldn't stop. It went on forever, waves and waves of spasms, the climax wringing her out until finally, she collapsed back on the bed.

She took a few moments to come back to herself. The mirror stared back at her, revealing nothing but her own exhausted form, until she finally rose to clean up and get dressed.

Sam met her in the hallway. He was waiting there, face flushed, cock a hard line in his pants. "Fuck," was all he said before pulling her into his arms and kissing her, hard.

They stumbled down the hallway back toward the bar, tumbling through the door into the bass-blasting music and patterned lights. A couch was open, and Sam was already pushing Abby down onto it before she could catch her breath.

"Can I fuck you?" he asked, already pulling at the hem of her dress. "I want to be inside you."

"Yes, God, yes." She had just come, but his desperation had her hot all over again. Sam freed his cock and rolled on a condom with fumbling fingers before thrusting, hard and long inside her.

It was messy, fast, frantic, and Abby could barely keep up, gasping for air as Sam fucked her hard on this couch. He reached between them to find her clit, still too sensitive, but the pain sparked inside her like pleasure, and she was climbing to orgasm again before she could catch her breath. She came in another rush of intensity, squeezing around his cock, and Sam groaned and cried out before coming inside her.

He sagged on top of her, and they both lay together, panting. Finally he said, "Holy shit."

Abby started laughing. She couldn't help it. She started

shoving at him, still chuckling. "Get off me. We've got to clean up."

. . .

They'd both lost their drinks somewhere along the way, so when they had recovered, Sam ordered them some new ones from the bartender, who didn't make a big deal at all out of the fact that he'd just seen them fuck like crazed animals on the couch in the corner of the room. He and Abby composed themselves and sat together on that couch, way more relaxed than before, drinking their drinks while the music thumped all around them.

"So." He twirled a strand of her long red hair around his finger, and she leaned into the touch, smiling lazily. "You having fun?"

"I'm doing all right." Her cheeky grin implied she was doing more than all right. "How about you? This living up to your fantasy?"

A twinge of guilt flickered in Sam's stomach. This wasn't one of his fantasies, not exactly. He'd chosen something sexy, something wild, something he'd been curious about, but it wasn't like he had been jerking off thinking of Abby at a sex club.

Although, after watching her through that two-way mirror, he'd be thinking of it in that situation a lot more in the future.

He let the lock of hair drop from his finger, then stroked his palm over the back of her head. "Everything I'd hoped for." It wasn't a lie; he'd hoped they would both have a good time, and this had far surpassed what he considered to be "a good time."

He'd had a sense about her exhibitionism kink, teasing it out through little hints, but she had been even more into it than he'd expected. They'd watched each other in the past, but never like this, never with this level of intensity and the public element. Now that he'd seen her perform, lose herself in the act of putting on a show, he wanted more of it.

Abby turned to face him more directly, pulling one leg up beneath her on the couch. She seemed to hesitate on this question for a moment before asking it. "Were you the only one watching me?"

He had been. He'd locked the door, actually, so no one else could come in. He'd done it out of instinct. But he hadn't told her that, and as several emotions flicked over her face, he considered his options. "Do you want me to tell you? Or do you want to imagine it how you wanted it?"

In the blue-tinted lighting of the room, her face still flushed. Interesting. She visibly mulled over the question before answering. "I…think I want to know."

He could lie. That normally wasn't in him; he wasn't the type of guy to lie about anything. Seeing her different emotions, though, the urge welled up inside him to fabricate an incredible story about a dozen people watching her, all of them hanging on her every move. That might be her fantasy, but actually, it was his. Realization hit him hard. He *wanted* other people to watch her. He shouldn't have locked the door. He should have let people in, because then he could have experienced the way they became as captivated with Abby as he was.

"I was alone."

She sagged slightly, relief and disappointment flickering over her expression in tiny micro movements of her eyes and mouth. With her mixed reactions, something lingered under there, the exhibitionism he'd been starting to understand.

"Do you wish I hadn't been alone?"

Abby averted her eyes, biting her lip. Obviously, the answer was no, based on her response, but he needed her to say it out loud. She'd been holding back a number of her fantasies, and this game was supposed to make her confess them. He needed the truth. Otherwise, how could he ever know if he was enough for her?

She brought her drink up to her lips and took a sip. She answered him, but it wasn't loud enough to be heard over the music, and he asked her to repeat it.

"I thought about other people being there." Her cheeks flushed darker. "It was kind of hot. I've never been watched like that before."

"What about the Campus Twenty?" She'd obviously performed for an audience in the past.

"That was about the guys. It's different when it's about me."

That made sense. "Right. Because when it's about you, you're the vulnerable one."

"Exactly." She nodded, relaxing a bit. "You get it."

"Do you like being vulnerable like that?"

Abby grinned and ducked her head again, which he had not expected. She was just full of surprises tonight, loosened up by the situation and maybe the alcohol. "Yeah, I do."

"I think it's hot." That was an understatement; her vulnerability jolted his arousal like an electric shock to his senses.

"Really?" She pursed her lips, dubious.

"Definitely." Watching her lie on that bed, head thrown back, whimpering as she held herself on the edge of climax, making herself wait...the thought of it made his cock twitch, even if he'd just come so hard he'd nearly blacked out.

Abby threw back another long swig of her drink and swallowed, the muscles of her throat drawing his eyes to her long neck. "You know," she said, "you're a surprising guy. I don't know how I feel about that."

"I don't know if I should be flattered or insulted."

Abby laughed. "That's fair. I don't know if I'm flattering you or insulting you."

He gave her a gentle shove, making her laugh more, and knocked back his own drink. This felt more like the Abby he knew, her fun and playful side, but less straitlaced than usual. This was the side of her he'd suspected beneath that composed veneer. His own fantasies, though, were a surprise: he'd never given much thought to voyeurism, and yet tonight was hotter than he'd imagined it could be.

"You know, the next fantasy is yours." He squeezed her thigh. "You thinking about what you're going to bring up?"

"I've been thinking about it." She tapped a finger against her lips.

"So many to choose from?" He tried not to sound nervous; if she brought up something really out there, he'd have some choices to make. He could go along with it, prove his open-mindedness to both of them, or he could admit that it was too much for him and live with the knowledge that they weren't sexually well-matched. The latter was untenable.

Abby made a noncommittal noise. "I have something in mind, but I don't think you'll go for it."

The challenge raised some competitive desire in Sam, adrenaline suddenly flooding his system. "Try me."

She was still considering, eyes narrowed in thought, her smile now more contemplative and a bit mischievous. "Okay. How about BDSM stuff?"

"Like what?" He may not know much, but he knew enough to know that there were a lot of different ideas wrapped up in that acronym. "You want me to tie you up and spank you or something?"

"I don't know, maybe." She shrugged. "But I was thinking more like…control. Like you tell me what to do and I have to obey you."

"I don't want to tell you do to stuff you don't want to do."

"No, not like that." She sighed. On the next couch over, a couple started undressing enthusiastically, mid make out, clothing pieces scattering everywhere. Abby gestured toward the door. "Can we go into the regular lounge?"

The regular lounge, with its street-legal clothing requirements and soft jazz, was a sensory reprieve after the thumping music of the bar. They found a corner with a soft leather sofa and sank into it together. Abby was still nursing her drink, and she took another sip before starting her explanation again, this time much quieter to suit the ambiance. "I wouldn't do stuff I wouldn't want to do. But it's kind of hot to be vulnerable, like we talked about before." She set her glass aside on an end table and twined her fingers together in her lap, shifting with nervous energy. "My fantasy is that you would be my Dom, for a little bit. You tell me what to do and I obey. I could always use a safe word, like 'red' or something, and we'd stop. It's just that sometimes I think about not being in control."

In the golden light of this room, her blush was much more prominent, the deep red of shyness indicating that yeah, this was her real fantasy.

He'd never given much thought to this kind of thing. BDSM was something other people did, people with leather and whips, who were really into pain. He wasn't really into pain, giving or receiving. Seeing Abby hurt would be a huge turnoff. And telling her what to do? What if she hated the idea of it? She'd said she could use a safe word, but even so, he'd have to take charge on everything. He would need to be firm with her, to tell her things and make her obey.

If he'd been in that room with her tonight, he could have been telling her what to do, commanding her to touch herself in a certain way. She would have obeyed him, yielding her pleasure to his wishes, trusting him to take care of her.

His cock twitched, just a bit, blood rushing into his too-sensitive shaft.

Oh.

"Okay."

Abby raised one eyebrow. "Okay? You'll do it?"

"Yes." He'd have to do some research, for sure, figure out more about this BDSM thing and what Abby might like. "But if you want to try this with me in the future, I think we should go to the dungeon now and watch."

Abby blinked, mouth open, and then picked up her drink and downed the rest of it in one gulp. She shivered, from the alcohol or from nerves, he couldn't be sure. "All right. Let's go."

The dungeon, ironically set up on the top floor instead of in the basement, had a posted list of rules next to the staircase that resembled the rules from the hostess, but more complete. There were additional regulations about medical play, needles, blood, stuff he didn't even want to contemplate because it was so far outside of his interests. But this baseline idea of commanding her and making her obey, he could do that. While they were in a building with an actual dungeon, they'd be foolish not to check it out.

The staircase opened up directly into an open loft space lit with dim red lighting, music steadily pumping through the space. The room was filled with furniture, different structures Sam didn't recognize but whose use was pretty obvious. A bench near them sat empty, and he stepped closer. The workmanship was solid, carved hardwood frame and smooth leather padding, metal eyelets for attaching cuffs.

Behind him, Abby started laughing, making him turn. "Did you seriously just examine the furniture before you noticed the naked people?"

Right, naked people. More than half the structures were occupied, a lot of action taking place all around them, and he'd checked out the bench. He had to laugh at himself. "I'm into design. I can't help it." He took her hand and pulled her over to an empty couch. "Come on. Let's sit and watch."

Most of the action in this room was impact related: moaning people were being hit with a variety of objects: hands, paddles, crops, other things he didn't know the names of. Most were bound. Off to one side, a woman was tying up her female partner in an elaborate rope harness, preparing to suspend her from a giant wooden frame. Sam's attention gravitated toward the neatness of her rope work, the smooth motions of her hands as she wove cord into knots.

"Is this something you've done before?" he asked. "Your other partners ever tie you up or spank you?"

"Not really." She shifted, leaning against him. Her whole demeanor was more relaxed than he'd expected, being surrounded by this kind of ambiance. "I had a boyfriend who'd spank my ass a little bit during sex, but it wasn't this kind of thing."

"So why do you think you'd like it?"

Abby paused, watching a couple over in the corner. She was tied to a large upright wooden X on the wall, blindfolded, her nipples weighted with painful-looking clamps. Her partner held a vibrator up between her legs, pressed against her, and her pleading became loud enough to hear as they watched.

"Please, Sir, please let me come," she sobbed, crying and twisting.

"No." He pulled the vibrator away, and she sagged in her bonds, her cries pitiful. After a moment, he pressed the toy against her once more.

She ratcheted quickly to the edge again, muscles tensing, back arching, and her thighs began to quiver. "Please," she begged once more. "Please let me come."

He pulled the vibrator away again. "No."

Next to him, Abby had gone very still. She watched with a kind of hypnotized expression, transfixed by the scene, and every muscle in her body was as tense as if she were the one experiencing this kind of torture. It was like she'd forgotten that he'd asked her a question. Maybe she'd forgotten he was even here. The man with the vibrator tortured the woman over and over, denying her five more times before she was a whimpering, incoherent mess. Then he took the toy away and began to stroke her with his fingers, light touches that also had her soon sobbing and writhing.

"What would you do to come?" he asked, loud enough for the room to hear.

"Anything," she begged, thrusting into his hand.

"When do you get to come?"

She responded immediately. "When it pleases you, Sir."

Abby's breath was shallow, her eyes dilated, hands clenched on her thighs as she watched them. In the time since they'd sat down, she'd sat up straighter, almost leaning forward, captivated.

Sam stroked a gentle hand down her back, reminding her that he was next to her, and she glanced over before looking back at the scene. She'd done this to herself, back in the room downstairs: held off her orgasm impossibly long. She wanted him to control her. Maybe he could do it like this. He could tease her, get her needy and desperate, just like the woman across the room right now, begging and squirming on the hands of that man. Her Dom. Abby was so controlled, even in her playfulness. He could take that control away from her, and she wanted him to do so. She'd shown hints of it before and now said it outright. He could strip that composed exterior down and make her submit. Thinking about this had him half hard again.

He leaned closer to Abby's ear. "You wish you were her?"

Abby's lust-blown eyes were all the confirmation he needed. "I don't know. Maybe."

"Do you like the thought of me controlling you like that?" Sam's heart had begun beating faster, too, knocking against his ribs.

Abby licked her lips. "Yeah. But I can't really picture it."

Of course she couldn't picture it. He'd been sweet, loving, and affectionate, ten years of compassion, and apparently that meant she couldn't see him as anything other than her caring husband. That was good, in so many ways. But he could see the appeal of deviating from that standard, shifting from her sweet lover to the controlling Dom who forced her to submit to more pleasure than she could take. And if it was out of his comfort zone? Fine. He could step outside his comfort zone and show her that she'd been underestimating him all this time.

The girl on the *X* sobbed again, and they both looked back toward the wall. "Do you think he'll let her come?" Sam asked.

"Fuck, I hope so," Abby said quietly. "I don't know how much more of this I can take."

On a hunch, Sam gathered a fistful of her hair. He squeezed at the root, pulling her hair just enough that she gasped and followed his hand. That took his dick from half-mast to fully hard. "I think you'll take it as long as I tell you to watch."

Abby gasped, an audible intake of breath so loud that someone nearby turned to look at them, but she had eyes only for Sam. Her lips twitched in a small smile. "Yes, Sir."

His grip slackened, a sudden flood of arousal taking his breath away. Those words sounded so good on her lips. Conflicting feelings rose up inside him: he shouldn't want her to submit, but he did; he wanted to feel that rush of power from knowing she would do what he told her.

"Suck my cock."

The words tumbled out, and Abby waited, like she still wanted to see if he meant them. Still with his hand in her hair, he squeezed once more, making her wince but also moan. He didn't like seeing her wince, but the moan went straight to his erection. With fumbling fingers, she undid his fly.

He hadn't expected to do this, definitely hadn't expected to push her mouth down onto his cock, but he was guiding her head before conscious thought caught up. Her mouth was sweet, hot, and so eager. He'd just come a little while ago, and his erection was too sensitive, almost painful, but he wanted this. He wanted to see what she would do.

Releasing his tight grip on her hair, he leaned back on the couch, trying to catch his breath as she worked him over. She looked so good bent over his lap, red hair spread across his trousers and the couch. The sense of control went right to his head, spinning up his arousal even faster than the sweet pressure of her mouth around his length.

Against the wall, the man had picked up the vibrator again and had it pressed between his crying partner's legs. Her begging sounded so sweet. Abby would sound so good like that, begging to come, raw and vulnerable and completely at his mercy. He'd never really thought about it before, and now, he rolled it over and over in his mind, losing himself in the multiple sensations of Abby's hot mouth and the other woman's sweet pleading, until he came in a gut-punch of pleasure that blanked out everything but overwhelming release.

Abby lifted her head off him, brushing her hair back, her lips swollen and red and her eyes wide with lust. They both watched as the Dom across the room finally, finally said "Yes" and let his partner come.

Abby sagged, turning her attention back to Sam as he

tucked himself back into his pants. "That was so hot," she said, eyes sparkling. "I'm soaking wet."

The idea came to him all at once. "I want you to stay that way."

Abby tipped her head to the side. "Okay?"

"I mean. Until I tell you otherwise, I don't want you to come."

Abby's mouth fell open. "But...I'm so turned on."

That little bit of neediness in her voice was so hot, even though he'd just come. She said she wanted to give up control, and he couldn't think of anything hotter than getting her worked up and desperate.

Maybe it was mean. This felt dark, building up her arousal and then keeping her from satisfying it. He wasn't a cruel guy. Normally, it wasn't in him to deny her even the slightest thing she wanted. She didn't ask for much, either, content in the day-to-day life they'd woven together.

But now, she'd revealed that she *did* want more. She wanted something kinky, and controlling, and naughtier than they'd ever done before. If she really wanted that, if she really wanted to submit to him, she was going to find out what that meant. Something controlling welled up inside him, the part of him that got hard thinking about her begging him for pleasure.

"I know you're turned on. I like it." He brushed her hair back and smiled. "Unless, of course, you'd rather call all this off. But if you want me to control you, then I'm going to control you."

Abby's eyes narrowed, and she smiled a wicked, challenging smile. "Yes, Sir."

Chapter Four

Abby had not been expecting Sam to go for this. BDSM was the thing he was going to balk at, the gentle, "Hon, that's too far" that she expected to hear. Yeah, it was one of her fantasies, but she'd brought it up in the first place because she'd half expected him to draw the line then. The other half of her had been secretly hoping he wouldn't, but she tried not to delve into that part of her mind that much. He was already shaking up her expectations. She didn't know how much more "other side of Sam" she was ready for.

Instead of being put off, though, he'd been *intrigued.* He'd suggested they go to the dungeon, of all places, and then he'd pulled out some grade-A mind fucking without any effort at all. Who the hell was this guy?

Worst of all, he hadn't brought it up again all week since they'd returned from their weekend in Boston. Every night before bed, he was reading *something,* and his only answer to her had been, "research."

Worst of all was not being able to come. She'd been so turned on, going down on him in the dungeon, and he'd forbidden her orgasm, lighting up her kinks like a Christmas tree. It was driving her crazy in the best way, but she was starting to get antsy. It had been a whole week, now, with no signs of him bringing it up again. She didn't even play with herself that much! Being told not to come, though, made her want it more than ever. Maybe he was waiting for her to ask. She'd considered asking him, last night, when she was lying in bed all twitchy and needy. But that felt like admitting defeat, and she wasn't about to do that. Instead, she suffered in silence, and had overwhelming sex dreams for the rest of the night. Today, Saturday, she'd been restless all day, and even some time at the pottery studio that morning hadn't calmed her down. He had to be gearing up for something tonight, right? God, she didn't want to wait any more days.

After dinner, when they were reading on the couch, he finally looked up from his tablet. His expression was neutral, calm, but her own nerves already had her jumpy. He looked her up and down and then nodded, like he was deciding something.

"Go in the other room, take off your clothes, and play with yourself."

Abby fumbled her book. Was he serious? She stared hard at him, because it wouldn't be difficult to imagine him suddenly laughing and telling her he was teasing. His face didn't imply teasing, though. He looked deadly serious.

"Do you not understand? Or are you not good at following orders?"

She blushed, heat rushing to her face, and set her book aside to go to the bedroom down the hall. He didn't follow her. Undressing alone, different emotions of embarrassment and curiosity warred for her attention. This felt silly, but she also wanted more of it. She wanted to see where this went. She left her clothes in a pile on the floor and, naked, stretched out on top of the comforter and lay back.

Her pussy was soaking already, and she hadn't even touched herself. Hadn't touched herself much at all this week, since touching herself would undoubtedly make it worse. Once or twice, she hadn't been able to resist, her fingers slipping over her sensitive clit and making her breath catch. Now, ordered to play, she lingered in slow, deliberate circles to draw out the feeling.

He hadn't given her permission to come. That detail nagged at her as she lay here, trying and failing to keep the thick pull of arousal at bay. He had told her to play with herself and not given any other instructions. He might not come in here at all. He might wait an hour, or more, letting her linger on the edge of orgasm without permission, and then tell her to come watch television. Fuck, he wouldn't do that, would he? She'd told him she was into that kind of control, so…he might.

The uncertainty sent shivers and tingles all throughout her body, as if the slow circles of her fingers against her clit weren't already doing that. This might kill her, this kind of anticipation without resolution. Maybe he knew that. Maybe he was better at this than he'd let on. Maybe instead of pushing him to his edge, getting him to admit he was out of his depth, she was the one out of her depth.

She hadn't even heard him come in until his soft voice said, "Good girl" from the doorway. Her eyes flashed open. He leaned against the doorjamb, calm, self-possessed, looking completely at ease. She lay there naked on the bed, and he stood fully clothed, watching her touch herself in quiet desperation and need. His gaze drew her in, locked with hers, and she couldn't look away, caught up in the magnetism until he broke the stare to come sit beside her on the bed.

The first touch of his fingertips through her hair hit her like a jolt. He brushed her red hair back from her face, back against the pillow. Her hand slowed between her legs as his actions distracted her. "Keep going," he said, not breaking eye contact. She obeyed, touching herself again. How could he look this passive, this dispassionate, when she was a worked-up ball of electricity?

"I've been doing a lot of reading this week." Sam continued to stroke Abby's hair, gentle caresses at odds with the burning need building in her blood. "I've been researching this fantasy of yours and how best to fulfill it. I've spent days looking into power exchange, reading blogs and stories, investigating different perspectives. You know I'm nothing if not thorough."

His comment made her smile, a bit of the tension easing. "It's true."

"Mmm." He lifted his chin. "Don't speak unless I ask you a question."

Oh *fuck*. She gasped, a stab of *please take me now* racing through her. Just that bit of control, being asked not to speak, and she was twitching at the edge of orgasm. She had to back off, slow her fingers on her clit, quiet her breathing. She couldn't ask to come. He hadn't given her permission. She was going to explode, and they hadn't even done anything yet.

"Good girl," he said again, and she flushed. "Do you like it when I say 'good girl'? Truthfully."

"Yes, Sir." She tried out the words, the honorific, and Sam smiled wider.

"I could get used to that." He looked her up and down. "Look at you. You're so beautiful. So flushed. I bet you want to come, don't you?"

He'd asked her a question. She could answer, but even answering feel like admitting too much. "Yes, Sir."

"Get close for me. Right to the edge of an orgasm. Tell me when you're there."

Being watched like this felt different than it had in the

sex club, where she couldn't see his expression. His intense focus, paying attention to nothing but her, broached a new level of intimacy, like her soul was naked rather than just her body. Tight, firm circles over her clit had her squirming, the pressure of a week's denial building up inside her until she had to ease up, her pussy already starting to twitch. "I'm there." Her eyelids slipped closed, her whole body centering in on this heavy pleasure thrumming deep inside her.

"Stay there for a minute. Don't come."

She loved and hated this, sitting on the precipice. Floating on the knife-edge of orgasm was a dangerous game. Too much pressure, and she might not be able to pull back in time; too little, and she craved more.

"Hands away."

Abby froze, opening her eyes to look at him. Really? She dragged her hands away from her soaking pussy, her clit pulsing with her heartbeat. Already, the orgasm ebbed away, fading from her senses, and she could have cried.

"How does that feel?" He picked up her hand by the wrist and held it, her fingers glistening with her wetness.

"Frustrating," she answered, then paused, because there was more. "Hot."

Sam slid her fingers into his mouth, his tongue sucking her juices away. Her pussy clenched around nothing. If only that tongue were between her legs.

He released her wrist. "Get to the edge again. Tell me when you're there."

She began to rub her clit once more, the arousal beginning to build.

"Do you like being told no?" he asked.

With the hormones surging through her blood, she would admit anything, but it still made her blush. "Yes. I like...oh, God...I like not knowing when you're going to let me come."

"Or if."

Shit. Normally she could read him so well, but he looked blank. Either he had been practicing this dominant act, or she'd just never seen this side of him. Whatever expression was on her face, it made him smile. "Took you by surprise there, hmm?" Reaching out, he rolled one nipple between his fingers, pinching it, sending another jolt into her body before he switched sides and did the same to the other. "I might decide to keep you like this, all strung out and needy."

"I'm there," she gasped, the delayed orgasm holding her whole body taut.

"Hands away."

Pulling away was torture, but she didn't want it to be easy, did she? That was the worst, and the best, knowing that she wanted to be tortured and he was doing it.

"Again."

He had her edge three more times, each one coming quicker than the last, and by the last one, she almost went too far and had to consciously relax all her muscles to keep from coming. This was insane. Her whole pussy was slick, her thighs, everything a mess.

Sam smiled thinly. This wasn't his normal smile. Something dark, something wicked looked out at her, an expression that turned her on and also scared the shit out of her. This man could be a total stranger. Was this all an act? Was he really getting off on this, or was he just putting it on for her benefit, because this was her fantasy?

"Tell me." He shifted on the bed. "Would you like more of this, or would you like something else?"

What the fuck would something else be? But if he kept edging her, she might go mad, or slip over the edge. "I don't know."

He got up and disappeared into the walk-in closet, returning after a moment with a coil of rope. Uncertainty and excitement bubbled up inside Abby, and she started to giggle, trembling on the bed. Sam smiled. "You like this?" He held it up.

Abby nodded, the giggles bordering on the edge of hysterics, and she tried to tamp them down. She'd never reacted like this before. Sam sat beside her again, smoothing her hair back, and leaned in to kiss her. "Are you okay?"

"Yeah. I mean, yes, Sir." She was more than okay. Her body was a continuous nerve, sensitive and needy.

"Okay. Good." He pinned both of her arms over her head and began to tie her wrists together. He'd been a Boy Scout; he tied quickly and efficiently, securing her wrists to each other and then to the headboard in a matter of moments. "Try to get away."

She couldn't. Pulling against the ropes, she lost her breath in a moment of panic, that sheer animal fear of being trapped. It passed, leaving her gasping and—how was it possible?—more turned on than before.

Sam stepped back from the bed and smiled at her bound form. Then he began to undress, methodical, quick, with businesslike precision. He folded his clothes and left them on the armchair in the corner, the one where he sometimes sat to read, the place where she'd also left her pile of clothes. Then, naked, he climbed into the space between her legs, carefully bending both knees back. Abby sucked in deep breaths, trying to steady herself, rubbing her wrists against the rope because it felt *so good* not to be able to get away.

Sam kept her knees pushed back and, slowly, nudged her slick entrance with his cock. *Please, more*, she wanted to beg, but couldn't find the words, and all the air left her lungs in a single moan as he thrust fully inside her.

He stayed buried all the way inside her, holding her hips, and his eyes fell half closed. "You feel...so tight, on the edge like this. *Fuck*." The swear sounded reverent on his lips, his expression a mixture of pleasure and restraint. Finally, he opened his eyes, more composed, and began to thrust.

Abby couldn't do much but lie there, each thrust opening her up to him. He pressed against her G-spot every time, sending little sparks through her body. He was using her, taking her body for his pleasure, moving harder and faster than she would normally want. Ah, damn, she loved it. She hadn't expected Sam to love it, too, but his face was a mask of bliss, lips parted, his hips moving like a man possessed. His steady, low exhales shifted to words, absolute filth tumbling out of his mouth.

"Damn, yes, look at you." He punctuated his words with hard thrusts. "So helpless. You just have to take it. Take what I give you. You can't get away."

Abby moaned, shifting as much as she could in this position. Sam was right. She couldn't get away, and that was the appeal of this, her own helplessness to whatever he wanted to do.

"Maybe I'll just have someone else come in, huh? Leave you here to get fucked by somebody else. Watch someone else enjoy your tight, sweet pussy. Would you like that?"

"Fuck," Abby cried, clenching reflexively around him. She'd had those fantasies, the ones she didn't admit to herself, fantasies of being taken by someone else. Sam might be just talking dirty, but she'd thought about that very thing, thought about it but would never say it out loud.

"Such a good girl," he groaned, and his fingers went to her clit, rubbing hard and pushing her right to that edge before she could fight it. "Ask me. Ask me to come."

She wanted it so bad, wanted that mind-melting pleasure, denied for so long. "Please," she gasped. "Please, may I come?"

"No." He pulled his hand away from her clit and grabbed her hips again. She could have cried, but she also loved it, loved this feeling of helplessness. Dual needs warred within her, the need to come and the need to please him. She couldn't stop clenching with every movement he made inside her, every thrust.

"So tight. You're such a good fuck. You're so hot, so wet, so perfect." His hips were moving erratically now, and he let go of her hips to lean forward, propping himself up above her, driving into her over and over again. "Anybody would be lucky, getting to come in this sweet cunt."

That right there almost pushed Abby over the edge. Sam so seldom swore, mostly during sex, never that crude, and somehow that mix of composed Sam talking filthy and fucking her without mercy had Abby shivering at the edge of orgasm, frantic to hold it off. She didn't even need his hand on her clit, now.

"Please, Sir, may I come?" Her voice had gotten higher, more desperate.

"I don't know." He leaned down and sucked one nipple into his mouth, and the contact raced through her like a straight line to her clit. "Do you like this? Tell me. Tell me the truth."

"Oh," she moaned, wincing, her breath coming shallow to her lungs. "Yes. I like…being helpless. And I like…you fucking me like this. And I like…shit, I like thinking about… about you watching someone else fuck me." The words tumbled out, confessions, desire so hot and thick in her blood that she was burning up from the inside out. "Please, Sir, please, may I come?"

Sam locked eyes with her, his expression feral and sharp, animal-like. "When I come, you can come."

She didn't know how much longer she could bear it, and she pulled against the ropes, thrashing, anything to distract herself from the deep, primal pull of her own release bearing down on her. Sam was merciless, hitting every tender spot in her pussy with brutal precision. Finally, he drove all the way inside her and held, coming hot and thick inside her, and Abby let herself fall over that impossible cliff into a climax that washed away all reality from her mind. Words dissolved and she was left gasping, crying, riding out this wave. He held steady, his cock still twitching inside her, until she sagged to the bed, everything fading away.

Abby came back to reality with Sam's weight heavy on top of her, the slickness of their combined wetness between her legs, a wash of discomfort and guilt settling all over her. Sam lifted off her, carefully, avoiding eye contact, and then moving up to untie her wrists with unsteady hands. Finally released, Abby flexed her fingers, touching the rawness where she'd rubbed her wrists red. She was cold. She curled up onto her side, drenched with sweat that was now cooling, and tried to wrangle her thoughts into something normal.

This wasn't normal, though. Something had shifted.

Sam had always been so gentle, so approachable, so nonthreatening. He hadn't been the kind of guy to shake her up. They'd rode this pattern for ten years now, but he wasn't that guy she'd expected. He'd acted like someone totally different. If this side of him was present all along, maybe she didn't know him at all.

• • •

Sam probably shouldn't leave Abby alone on the bed, not after what they'd just done, but he stood in the bathroom way longer than it took to use it, staring at himself in the mirror. Shit, what had he just *said*? He'd had a sense of how he wanted tonight to go. He'd planned on teasing her, bringing her to the edge of orgasm a few times, tying her up, and making her come. He hadn't planned on spilling out all this dirty, filthy confessional stuff, ideas he hadn't even really thought through. And now, there they were, out in the open.

Abby was curled up on the bed, and he put a hand on her back. Her skin felt cold and clammy. "Hey. Why don't we take a shower together?"

Abby pushed herself up onto one elbow and looked up at him, hesitant. "Sure," she said at last. "Sure."

Showering together was this baseline kind of connection that always made Sam feel close to Abby. Even though their shower wasn't big enough to make this sort of thing comfortable, it wasn't really about getting clean. He steered her under the water and began to rinse her hair. She tipped her head back and closed her eyes.

He needed to say something. "I hope that was okay."

Abby picked her head up, raising her eyebrows. "Okay?" She started to laugh. "Yeah, clearly I was enjoying myself."

"I didn't want to go too far. I hope I didn't go too far. I got a little carried away there." He poured some of her shampoo into his hand and began to lather up the thick red locks. She smiled, leaning into his touch, already visibly relaxing.

"It's fine. I got a little carried away, too. It's normal." She was comforting him, here, and he should really be comforting her.

"You were so incredible tonight."

Abby wrinkled her nose, bashful, and closed her eyes as Sam began to rinse her hair with the warm water. "Thanks?" She sounded hesitant. "I didn't do much but just lie there."

He waited to say anything else while the water was running over her head. How could he even put into words the way he'd felt about her responses? She came out from under the water, and he picked up the conditioner. "I know this was your fantasy," he said, "but I feel more like you were tapping into one of mine."

"Oh?" She tipped her head to the side as he added conditioner to her long locks. "I guess that's good, right? Like the sex club. It's good when we both enjoy ourselves."

"So you enjoyed yourself, too." He needed to confirm.

"Yeah, I already said that." She laughed. "You were a little surprising, though."

It would probably seem that way to her, for sure. "I don't know what I was saying, there." The words were all coming back to him in waves, memories that embarrassed him even as much as they still turned him on. "I don't...like to use language like that."

Abby reached for the body wash, but he took it from her, squirting it onto her mesh sponge so he could wash her. Running his hands over her body like this, touching her tenderly, seemed to offset some of the cognitive dissonance about his previous actions. "What language?" she asked. When he hesitated, she guessed. "Cunt?"

"Yeah." He never used that word, knew how offensive it could be. "I'm sorry."

Now, she outright laughed, and he wasn't expecting that. "Don't apologize. It was hot. Dirty talk is hot."

"Right. Okay." Good, so she wasn't offended. He should apologize for the rest of it, too, the parts about seeing her fucking other guys, play all that off to fantasy. Even as he went to open his mouth and say it, though, something stopped him. He couldn't blame that on getting carried away. He *had* been fantasizing about that, and more than just tonight. His mind had been turning it over and over ever since the reunion, when he'd first found out some details from her past.

He closed his mouth, kept washing her, turning away from eye contact. Guilt simmered in his stomach. He couldn't deny that tonight was hot. He didn't want to undo anything that had happened. But it was all said, now; everything was out in the open, for better or worse. She might pretend none of it mattered, but that didn't undo it.

And he didn't want to undo it. He'd loved every minute of this, even when she was desperate and begging him. She came undone, and he reveled in it.

"I feel like I should be washing you," Abby said, her voice loud after the silence that had fallen between them.

"Huh?" He rinsed the sponge off under the water.

"You know. Serving you and all that." She gestured toward the bedroom. He followed her gesture, even though that direction was only shower curtain.

"Oh. That's…over. That's not…that was just…"

"I know." She smiled. "It wasn't real. It was just a fantasy." She stepped under the stream of water and began to rinse the suds from her body. He couldn't even argue with her, because she was giving him the benefit of the doubt. She'd taken this to just be him, enjoying himself while fulfilling her fantasy. She had no way of knowing how turned on he'd been all week, thinking about this type of control. He'd gotten hard every night, seeing her shift in her sleep, her hips moving in sleepy arousal. A few times, he'd jerked off in the shower, so turned on by her frustration and this heady sense of power over her. He couldn't get this needy, desperate Abby out of his head, and shit, he didn't want to.

What kind of a man was he, if he loved taking control of her this much? She'd yielded so beautifully and had apparently enjoyed herself immensely in the process. Sure, she was smiling now, rinsing the conditioner from her hair, sated and content. But they couldn't take back what had been said and done. Things were different between them, and they couldn't go back to the way they'd been together before this all began.

Abby opened her eyes and pulled him close, oblivious to the turmoil inside him. "Come on. It's my turn to wash you."

• • •

Sam let the kettlebell hit the ground with a lot more force

than normal, the jolt vibrating up his arms, and he shook them out and unclenched his hands. His muscles were doing that trembly, Jell-O-like thing when he'd been working out too much, but at some point, working out this hard was going to make the unsettled, anxious feelings go away. It always worked. He could come here to CrossFit, bust his ass, and end up feeling way better than when he went in. Tonight, though, all he was getting was sore.

He hadn't seen Mitchell come up next to him, but suddenly the guy was there, doing effortless pull-ups on the pull-up bar. Mitchell moved quietly, too quietly for his size, and had a propensity for sneaking up on people. He was also watching Sam. That was weird. Mitchell kept to himself a lot of the time, chatting with the guys when they went out for drinks, but not usually opening up very much and definitely not usually staring down Sam like he was a project that needed solving.

"Hey," Mitchell said. He paused, hanging from the pull-up bar, and then dropped down to the ground. "You okay?"

So apparently it was that obvious. Sam flushed. "Yeah. I'm fine. Just got a lot on my mind."

Mitchell made a soft "hmm" noise. "Want to get a drink after the workout?"

Sam didn't exactly want to go and talk about his feelings, but it would be nice to have some company, since Abby was at pottery tonight. When he hesitated, Mitchell added, "I'm trying to avoid doing some kitchen prep work for the week, and it would be nice to have an excuse."

So Sam rolled into the Night Owl after his workout to see Mitchell already there, sitting at the bar, empty chairs on either side of him and a glass of Scotch whisky in front.

Sam pulled up the chair next to him and leaned on the bar. His hair was still wet from the gym shower, and tiny curls of ice clung to its ends from the freezing walk in from his parking spot. "Whisky again?"

Mitchell nodded, giving a little half smile. "It felt like a nice indulgence on a cold night like this." He looked out at the night, the dark windows with the lights of Main Street beyond. "We've been lucky for snow so far."

Sam ordered an Old Fashioned from the bartender when she came over. "I don't mind the snow. Abby and I try to go skiing as often as we can, but lately, the skiing season's been getting shorter and shorter." He sighed, folding his arms on the bar.

Mitchell tipped back his whisky, the amber liquid rushing past the ice cubes into his mouth. He grimaced and swallowed. "You an Old Fashioned kind of guy?" At Sam's blank stare, he gestured to the bartender. "The drink."

"Oh. Right. Yeah, I like it." He chuckled at a memory. "Abby used to tease me about it. Every time I ordered one, she'd tell me I'm, and I quote, 'really fucking old.'" Those were back in the days when they were dating, when everything had seemed simpler.

"That what's got you working yourself into the ground tonight? Something going on with Abby?" Mitchell glanced over as the bartender set the Old Fashioned down in front of Sam, then turned back to his own drink and nursed another sip.

Sam drank the Old Fashioned, tipped it back and downed half in one gulp. It burned all the way down, up into his sinuses and down his throat. He hadn't eaten much, just a sandwich after work before going to the gym, and maybe that was a mistake. It didn't stop him from taking another large gulp from the glass. "I don't know. Things are confusing. Got a lot on my mind." He finished the drink in one. There it was, the soft hum of alcohol in his system. He got the bartender's attention and ordered a second.

Mitchell raised an eyebrow. "You aren't gonna drink like that and drive." It wasn't a question.

"Nah." Sam shook his head. "I'm in overnight parking the next lot over. I can just take a cab." The prospect of letting alcohol fuzz through his system was too good to pass up.

The bartender brought him a second drink, which he downed as quickly as the first, and then ordered some tequila shots. "How about some food?" she asked. "Some nachos? Fries?"

"Sure. Nachos." That would be fine.

"Don't worry, Bella," Mitchell reassured her. "He tries to drive and I'll beat the shit out of him."

Bella laughed. "You both take it easy. It's a quiet night. Don't want you getting all rowdy up in here."

She walked away, and Mitchell let him take both tequila shots. "All right," Mitchell repeated. "You aren't a heavy drinking guy. Wanna tell me what's up?"

"I don't know, man." Sam was fuzzy all through his brain. "I don't know. This is personal shit. Stuff. I'm sorry for swearing."

Mitchell laughed. "It's fine. I don't care if you swear. I'm not a priest. I'm pretty far from a priest, to tell you the truth."

Whatever that meant. "I don't want to overshare or get all weird or something."

Mitchell shrugged. "Listen, Sam. I've got nothing better going on right now, and you look like you're in a bad way."

"See, I'm not." That was the weirdest part about it. "I'm not in a bad way. I'm just..." Well, he might as well get into this. "You ever think you understand everything about yourself, and then something comes along and just shakes you right down to your core? Like, you realize everything you knew about yourself was incomplete, there was this whole other half just, just there?"

Mitchell smiled, this amused smile, like Sam had just told a great joke. "You've got no idea."

That wasn't the reaction he'd been expecting at all. Come

to think of it, he didn't really *know* Mitchell that well, aside from work and CrossFit and some drinks, and he'd have described them as friends, but they didn't share anything super personal. They talked exclusively about distant stuff, stuff unconnected to their personal lives beyond the superficial. He blinked at Mitchell, taken aback. "Okay. Well…I'm going through that right now. Been going through it all week."

"It's hard, reevaluating yourself. You want to get more specific, or talk generally?"

Sam looked around. There was nobody there. "It's sex stuff."

Mitchell snorted. "Yeah, I figured. So, what? You figure out you're not straight or something?"

"No, nothing that extreme." He shifted on his chair. "So it started at Abby's college reunion, when I find out she used to be this whole different person. Somebody she doesn't think I'd like, because she used to be way more…I don't know, sexually adventurous." And he told the story, about making the bet, about wanting to show her that he could handle whatever she could throw at him, about them exchanging fantasies. Nachos showed up, and he split them with Mitchell, who helped himself. The nachos were a good choice, because he had been fucking starving. Normally, empty carbs and cheese weren't his plan of attack, but there was something about nachos that really hit the spot tonight.

"Anyway, she said she wanted to try something kinky. Some BDSM stuff. Wants me to be her Dom. And we fooled around with this, last weekend."

He paused. There were several ways to get further into this story, and another Old Fashioned had shown up (Had he ordered that? He must have.) so he drank a little of it while he considered.

"And you discovered you really liked it." Again, not a question from Mitchell, a statement.

"Yeah. I *really* liked it. It blew my fucking mind. But now I don't know how to even *be* with Abby, because I know she liked it too, and that feels…different. Like we've had this shift in how we are together." He sagged, pulling a nacho off the plate and popping it into his mouth. "I don't know what comes next."

Mitchell made a thoughtful noise. He did that a lot, those contemplative noises. "How does it change who you are together?"

"Because there's this whole power exchange thing just, just hanging out there. And what if she wants more of it?"

"You liked it," Mitchell reminded him. "You can just have more of it."

"But I didn't even know I was *like* this." Sam sighed, tipping his head back. "I can't believe I'm even talking about this shit. Out loud. In public. To you." He had some more of his drink. "Don't judge me. I'm not a deviant."

Mitchell laughed. He didn't laugh much, not that kind of open-mouthed, earnest laugh, but he clearly wasn't laughing at Sam. He was laughing…with him? He definitely seemed amused at himself, not at Sam, and Sam was missing something here.

"Listen. Sam." Mitchell patted Sam's shoulder. "You're overthinking this, man. It's just kink. It's only as serious as you want it to be. You like giving your wife orders, you both get off on it, great. Do it. You're both happy with it. It doesn't have to change anything else." At Sam's dubious look, he went on. "You don't have to start wearing leather clothes and get her a collar and a leash." He paused. "Unless you're both into that."

"But it's a whole identity thing," Sam reiterated. "I don't know who I am anymore. I started all this to show Abby that I could keep up with her. I didn't think I'd get so into it."

"Seems like that doesn't have to be a bad thing." Mitchell

shrugged. He stared up at the bottles behind the bar, mouth set, and finally nodded as he seemed to make up his mind about something.

"Sam, I'm a Dominant."

Sam stared at him. Mitchell had spoken low, low enough that only Sam could hear, which was a good reminder that the bar wasn't super busy and they should keep their voices down. Sam had a tendency to get loud when he was drunk.

Mitchell waited for some kind of response, and when it didn't come, he tipped his head. "Like you. I'm into that. It's what I do. It's my main sexual kink. I like to dominate the people I have sex with, if they like being dominated."

"Oh." That actually made a lot of sense. Mitchell was a quietly in-control kind of guy. Sam, though? "I'm not really the dominant type," Sam said. At Mitchell's raised eyebrow, he explained. "I'm in control at work. I like order and structure. But it's not like I like being bossy or something."

"See, I do like being bossy, but that's just my personality. The way you are in the sack and the way you are in the rest of your life don't have to overlap with each other." Mitchell shrugged. He pursed his lips and then sighed. "Sam. Lots of people discover things about themselves in their thirties. It's common. Just a few months ago, I realized I was in love with two people."

Sam gawked. "What?"

"Yeah." Mitchell gestured toward the windows, as if the people he loved were standing right out there, which of course they weren't. "I'm polyamorous. We all are. Me, and Ben, and Hannah."

"What the hell?" Sam couldn't keep the disbelief out of his voice. "Nobody does that."

"Yeah, people do. We do that." Mitchell was actually fully smiling now. "And it turns out a lot of people do that. We have a discussion group about it here in Mapleton. We meet once a month or so, talk about how to have open relationships, or sleep with other people, or have a relationship with more than two."

"Do I know Hannah?" Sam was trying to think about who he'd seen Mitchell with. He seldom saw Mitchell outside the restaurant or gym, but maybe he'd seen her at the restaurant.

"My height, curvy, brown hair, wears librarian glasses?" Mitchell shifted in his chair. "She also runs the sex shop Yes Please, the one right next to the restaurant."

"I don't know her, I don't think." Sam was still gawking. "I can't believe you're doing this and I didn't even know about it. That is…unbelievable."

"It's a lot of people's fantasies, for sure." Mitchell smiled sheepishly.

Fantasies, right. That snapped Sam back to the conversation. "That's the other thing. I have been having all these fantasies about Abby with other people. I think it started back at the reunion, when this all first came up." He ate some more nachos, and then took the glass of water that Mitchell had ordered for him.

"That's a pretty common fantasy." Mitchell finished the last of the nachos. "I think it's called hotwifing. Is it something Abby's interested in doing?"

"I haven't told her." Sam shook his head. "That feels way too far. Even the thought of bringing it up, it's like, I can't imagine being someone who has these thoughts in the first place, let alone sharing them. It's like I'm not the man she married."

Mitchell shrugged. "You're not. You're changing. We're all changing. It's life, man. It's what we do." Mitchell finally finished the last of his whisky, the same glass he'd somehow been drinking this whole conversation while Sam pounded the booze. "You think it was easy, realizing I wanted more than one person in my life, forever? Falling in love with them?

I've been in love with Ben for years, and having to confront that, it was scary shit. It's still scary. I don't know what's going to happen with us, but I want to have them both in my life. Once I realized that, it got a lot easier."

Mitchell, the Dominant, in a relationship with two people at once. Sam really didn't know this guy at all. "You're kind of rocking my worldview, here."

"It's not that complicated." Mitchell shrugged. "I get it. I tend to make things complicated. Ben's always after me to think simpler. You want to be with Abby, obviously, and you want to have this kinky sex and explore this different side of your relationship, go for it. See where it leads."

"And what about…" Sam hesitated. "What about if we go past just the two of us?"

"What, another person? A threesome?" Mitchell leaned back in his chair. "Bring it up with her. Maybe she'll think it's hot, too. Seems like you're both batting a thousand when it comes to fantasies."

"Are we going too far, though?" That was the other question eating at his brain.

"For what? For hot sex? It's just sex, Sam." Mitchell ate a jalapeño that had fallen off the nachos onto the bare plate. "Just fuck like you want to fuck. Don't make a big deal out of it. It's only as significant as you make it, together. It can just be fun."

"Right." He wasn't really convinced, but Mitchell was speaking some sense, for sure. Maybe it could be this simple. Abby was into being watched, clearly, her exhibitionism rising up at new points, and he could play with that. He could tease her, and they could have fun together.

"And listen. You're gonna find out new things about yourself. It's okay. Let it happen. Growth, man. Growth." He clapped Sam on the back. "You want me to drive you home?"

"Actually." Sam was getting another idea. "You said there's a sex shop, Yes Please. How late are they open?"

Chapter Five

Sam was normally a pretty easy guy to read. He was straightforward with his feelings, up-front when he was having a bad day or needed some time to himself, a completely open book that Abby could read without trouble. For the last week, though, ever since what she'd been thinking of as Kink Night, he'd been…reserved. Normally, she wouldn't have read too much into it. She'd tell herself that he was busy at work, and he probably was, but she wouldn't dwell on it longer than that. Now, with whatever this "give a fantasy, get a fantasy" game they had been playing, she kept ruminating on every action of his like it might mean way more than she expected. After all, it was his turn to share a fantasy, and he'd given no sign of wanting to do anything else. In fact, up until going to the gym last night, he'd been mopey as hell, and then he'd come home late via cab, drunk on a weeknight. It wasn't like him.

So, sitting at dinner that Friday night, Abby geared up toward ending their game. She'd been rehearsing the speech in the mirror, about how he was obviously upset after playing with power exchange, and they'd gotten in over their heads too fast, and he would clearly be happier if they went back to the way things used to be. She wasn't even going to talk about how the whole "fantasy swap" had been a bad idea that he hadn't been ready for. She took a deep breath, and let it out.

"So I've been thinking."

Sam paused, his fork halfway to his mouth, and then carefully finished his bite before setting down the fork and chewing. He had that wide-eyed innocent look that meant she was taking him totally by surprise.

"I know you're upset about the way things went last weekend," she began, ready to segue into the part about calling everything off.

Sam interrupted her, still giving her that wide-eyed, taken-aback stare. "I'm not upset."

Bullshit. "You've been distant all week. You've been kind of weird ever since we did it. Like you've got a secret." She paused, and he spoke into the silence.

"I look like I've got a secret because I've got a secret." He smiled, taking another bite of his dinner.

What? Sam was shit at keeping secrets. He got too excited about buying her presents and always wanted to give them to her early, having more fun watching her on Christmas morning (or Christmas Eve, if he couldn't wait) than he did opening his own gifts.

As if reading her mind, he added, "You know I'm awful at keeping secrets."

"What's the secret?" Abby set down her own fork.

Sam shook his head. "After dinner. It's part of the fantasy I want to share with you."

What the hell? She had not expected him to be ready to share a fantasy, not after being weird all week.

"You've been weird all week about this. Now you're saying it's fine?"

Sam shrugged. "I had a talk with Mitchell from the gym.

He helped me figure some stuff out that had been bothering me." He gestured to her plate. "Aren't you gonna have any more? It's really delicious."

Boggling, Abby narrowed her eyes, mouth open in confusion. "So you're just fine now?"

Sam tipped his head to the side. "I don't know if I'm fine, but I'm better than I was. And I want to keep going, because I'm having a really good time fulfilling fantasies with you."

Was he telling the truth? She scrutinized him.

"I'm not lying," he insisted. Damn, he was too good at knowing what she was thinking when it came to things like this. "I really do have another fantasy I want to share with you."

"Another one?" She'd been ready for him to want to wait a while.

He laughed. "Yeah, another one. You think I just have the one, that sex club fantasy, and that was it?"

"Is that what your secret is?"

"Partially." He hesitated. "I'll show you after dinner."

After dinner, she followed him into the bedroom and joined him on the edge of the bed, anticipation already zinging down her spine. "You remember how we used to go out dancing all the time when we were dating?" he asked.

"Yeah." It had been one of their favorite hobbies. "We stopped when you broke your foot."

"And never got back to it." He looked tense, expectant. "I want us to go out dancing again."

There had to be something more to this than that. Dancing wasn't a fantasy; it was something they used to do. "Tonight?"

"Yeah. Tonight." He pulled a small box out of his nightstand drawer and held it close to his body, obscuring whatever the labeling said, before handing it to her. "And I want you to wear this."

The white box pictured a curved, *U*-shaped teal device. Puzzled, she opened the box, and a silicone toy tumbled into her lap. She pushed and held the only button it seemed to have, and it buzzed once in her hand, making her drop it back on her lap.

Oh.

Oh.

Sam's expression told her all she needed to know, and the blush radiated from her face down her neck. She gingerly picked up the vibrator, holding it between her thumb and forefinger. "You want me to wear this out tonight when we go dancing?"

"Yeah." He licked his lips, and his eyes had gone dark. "Babe. I know you like showing off. I know it makes you hot when people are watching you. I want to know if it makes you hot if I'm the only one who knows you're wearing a vibrator."

"Shit." Her hand closed around the toy. "Won't someone hear it?"

"Not at Heads or Tails. Not with the music that loud."

Heads or Tails was always a popular salsa dancing club, their favorite place to get a little rowdy, two towns over from Mapleton and drawing a livelier crowd.

Just the idea of this was turning her on. "How do I wear it?" she asked.

"Take off your clothes."

Abby undressed, heart beginning to race in her chest. She hadn't been clubbing in years, and had never done anything like this before. When she was naked, Sam pushed her back on the bed, leaning over her to kiss her waiting mouth. God, he could kiss, his lips on hers making everything else fade away, up until his fingers brushed up through her folds and found her clit.

She jumped. The contact hit her like an electric shock, not altogether pleasant, just abrupt. Sam pulled back. "Seems like you should warm up a little bit, first, yeah?"

Before she could say yes, he crawled down her body and got between her legs. Oh, shit, she closed her eyes and bit her lip, bracing herself for that first touch, arousal ratcheting up from three to ten just at the light brush of air on her clit.

And he waited.

She opened her eyes, looking down her body. Sam was kneeling there, meeting her eyes, just waiting with a smile on his face. He waited until she looked at him and then licked her clit.

"Shit!" she cried out, and he laughed, the motion making his mouth vibrate her skin. Getting head from him was nearly too much, the kind of fierce overwhelming pleasure that consumed her. He only had to start licking her and she was already dripping wet, sensation running up through her body and radiating from her clit outward.

"There we go." He sat back and dragged his fingers through her now-wet folds. "It's important to warm up."

"You asshole." She threw a hand over her head. "Do we have to go dancing? Can't we stay here?"

"We can, sure. Is that what you want?" He circled her clit with two slick fingers.

Fuck him for calling her bluff. She sighed. "No."

"Good girl."

The words made her blush again, that jerk, but she had to smile. Her smile faded with an intake of breath as a blunt pressure pushed against her pussy. The toy slid in place, half of the *U* penetrating her to push against her G-spot. The other part of the toy lined up between her folds, snug between her labia, the tip nestled firmly over her clitoris. Sam tapped it, and it settled perfectly against her. "There we go. You can sit up."

Abby pushed up to her elbows, cautiously, then sat all the way up. The toy moved with her, a constant pressure but no stimulating vibration, not yet.

"Put on some very snug panties, I think." He winked at her and watched as she carefully got up to do so.

She had just pulled on some lacy panties, slipping them all the way up over her hips, when the vibrator came to life against and inside her. She gasped, then clapped a hand over her mouth to muffle the gasp, and spun to see Sam. He had his phone out. Holy shit, he could control it with his phone.

"Looks like it works." He dragged his fingers up the screen, and the vibration ratcheted up, pleasure coursing through her clit and all throughout her body like a sudden live wire. She gripped the bureau to steady herself.

"Holy fuck." She released her grip as the vibration turned off.

"Seems perfect." He smiled, devilish. "We should both get dressed."

Heads or Tails was the kind of club that drew a fashionable crowd, and Abby settled on a blue dress with a lot of flow to it, the kind that would twirl along with her. Sam kept the toy off the entire time they were getting ready, but it still pressed against her, rubbing her clit each time she moved, reminding her it was there. When her hair and makeup was done, and they were both ready to leave, the vibrator came to life once more, low and quiet. She froze.

"I just want to make sure you can move all right while wearing it." He smiled, innocent and sweet, like he wasn't about to torment her in public with a secret sex toy. "After all, you shouldn't get caught with it, right?"

"You know this is going to kill me." She composed herself and dropped her head back. "But I'm going to hide it."

"Good girl."

She rounded on him. "You cannot keep saying that. It turns me on every time."

Sam backed her up against the door, suddenly, firmly,

pinning her against it with his body. Her pussy clenched in reflex, squeezing the part of the vibrator tucked inside her, and she gasped out loud. This moment, the toy, his smoldering expression, that tiny bit of *fear* she suddenly felt, all of it cranked her arousal up another five notches.

He read the expression on her face, that gasp, and smiled. "I like having you turned on." Leaning closer, he kissed her again.

Fuck, they did not need to leave this house. They could stay right here, and Abby would melt into Sam and let him turn that vibrator all the way up and come and come and come. But no. He broke the kiss, pulled back, and squeezed her ass. "I think I should drive."

He did eventually turn the toy off, hitting a button on his phone when they were stopped at a red light just outside of town, giving Abby a breather until they arrived at the club. Even in the depths of winter, in the late January darkness, Heads or Tails was pulsing with music and overflowing with people. Just walking through the front door took Abby back ten years in a heartbeat.

Sam slid an arm around her waist. "Memories, right?"

"So many." She let him lead her up to the bar. "Drinks first?"

Sam ordered an Old Fashioned, because of course he did, and ordered a Bellini for her, knowing her penchant for peach and fizzy drinks. "You're really fucking old, you know," she shouted, loud enough to be heard over the music, pointing at his drink.

Sam smiled, the corners of his eyes crinkling. "You remember when you used to make me guess what drinks you wanted to order? And you always told me whatever I picked was exactly what you wanted."

"And then you figured me out." Abby started laughing, the memory coming back all at once. "So you started ordering really horrible shit, trying to get me to admit I was lying about it being exactly what I wanted."

"And I'd drink it all for you." He looked younger, happier, lighter than she'd seen him in months. How had she ever thought he'd been upset about this? This game was the most fun they'd had in a while.

She drank some more of her Bellini, the bubbles fizzing up into her nose, taking increasingly long swigs until she downed the entire drink and set her glass on the bar. "Come on and dance with me." She grabbed his hand. He tossed back the rest of his drink and did.

Of course, as soon as she moved into his arms, the pulsing beat of the music flowing through them, he pushed a button on the phone in his pocket and the vibrator started. Not high, not all the way up, but stronger than it had been, strong enough to soften her knees and make her wobble against him. He caught her, holding her close, pulling her against him. "There we go. Dance with me, sweetheart."

Each shift of her hips, each gyrating movement, pushed the vibrator further against her. It moved with her like it was attached, stimulating her mercilessly. Was this really happening? Was she really getting teased by Sam, in a public place, where bodies pressed in on all sides and nobody could tell what was happening? She couldn't move away from the vibration because it was snug against her, as tightly as Sam was, the music pulsing and her clit throbbing beneath the vibrator that clicked her arousal higher and higher.

"Please," she breathed, and he must be able to see the word on her lips even if he couldn't hear her over this music. He reached into his pocket and…the vibrator went up higher.

Fuck. She gasped loud enough that he could probably hear her, probably multiple people could hear her. His expression was so pleased, so smug, so confident. Jesus, this side of him had been here all along, hiding beneath his calm exterior, and he was going to make her come in the middle of this dance floor.

She mutely blinked up at him, all her words gone. He was watching her, watching this happen, watching what her face looked like when the climax began to build in her body. Leaning down, he brushed his lips against her ear. "I want to watch you come like this." He dipped her back and moved against her, encouraging the rocking of her hips, the desperate desire for more stimulation that might look to anyone else just like some particularly close dancing.

She could not hold out any longer. Her muscles tensed, and clinging to Sam's shirt, she came with a single slow, shaky exhale. Her pussy spasmed intensely, clenching and clenching around this one small toy, clit twitching beneath the relentless vibration that would not let her down. Sam watched her with his lips parted and eyes half closed, so clearly turned on. His arousal was as hot as the situation. He definitely loved watching her. He loved watching this, watching her lose control, loved every moment of this display she was putting on only for him.

He dropped his hand into his pocket once more and the vibrator stopped, giving her sensitive nerves a rest, and she sagged against him, supported by his arm. "Let's go sit," he murmured, unnecessarily, because she was obviously going to need to sit down.

"Holy hell." She sank down onto one of the couches in the corner, where people gathered to talk a little farther away from the dancing. Her heart pounded hard against her ribs, thrumming, slowly regulating along with her breathing. Sam sat close by her side, his arm over her shoulders.

"That was so sexy." He kissed her, just like that, right in the middle of the club, open-mouthed and filthy hot. She may have just come, but she was in the mood to fuck him right here if it wouldn't get them both arrested.

"I am a mess." She giggled against his mouth, dizzy and light-headed. "I need some air. Or water."

"You want to go outside?" He gestured to the door.

"Nah, but maybe get me some water?"

Sam went to do so, and Abby was left sitting on the couch, getting her bearings. She looked around the club. Back when they were younger, they'd meet friends here. It wouldn't be unusual to see someone she recognized. She hadn't wanted to look too closely before, what with the circumstances, but now she had recovered somewhat and was able to focus on something other than her clit.

Well, fuck.

Zachary Levine sat leaning on the bar, chatting in his amiable way with the very handsome bartender. She hadn't seen him before, but she hadn't been looking. Had he been there the whole time? The club was crowded, and they had been caught up in a sea of people. Now, she was a direct line of sight to him, this man she hadn't seen since college and then, suddenly, saw twice in one month.

Sam was at that same bar, getting her water, and they didn't seem to notice each other. There were a number of people between them, so that made sense; the whole club was busy on a Friday night. Sam got her glass of ice water and another drink for himself and sat down next to her on the couch, handing her glass over to her.

"Zach is at the bar." She tried to sound normal, casual, like she was making an observation. "Zachary Levine. From the reunion." She took a minute to sip some of her water. Her head didn't feel clearer now; it felt foggy, like the presence of Zach had confused her all over again when she was just starting to clear up. What the hell?

Sam followed her gaze toward the bar. He tensed up. They'd watched Zach have sex with someone at the reunion. They'd laughed and joked and told old stories, and then Zach had gone onto the porch to fuck another woman and they'd watched and both gotten hot over it. Sam had said he was okay. He'd said it turned him on. That had started this whole "share a fantasy" thing they were doing, this game that was quickly becoming more consuming all the time. Maybe Sam had changed his mind. Maybe seeing Zach was bringing up some feelings in him.

"You should go visit with him." Sam leaned back on the couch.

"What?" She looked from Sam to Zach and then back to Sam.

Sam licked his lips. "Dance with him."

"I don't…" She stopped. This was weird. "I don't have feelings for Zach like that. I'm with you. I'm married to you."

Sam turned a little pink. It was hard to tell, with the lights in the club changing, but he was definitely blushing. What the hell?

"I like to watch you flirt," he admitted. "It's hot. I want to see you flirt with Zach. If… I mean, if you're comfortable with it."

Fuck, she shouldn't want that. She shouldn't want to go over and flirt with Zach. She was a married woman. She was happy with Sam. Zach was all the things she'd left behind. This wasn't just voyeurism, this was something more, something on the verge of indecency, and the desire ramping up in her body was dangerous.

At her silence, he continued. "You don't have to, if it makes you uncomfortable. But if you're just worried about me, I…" He trailed off, then closed his eyes, gathering his resolve before he opened them again. "It really turns me on. Watching you, watching you flirt with him, I…I want to see that."

Sam had said some pretty filthy things in the midst of Kink Night last week, stuff about seeing another man fucking her. She'd chalked it up to dirty talk, but maybe there was some truth underneath it all. And if he wanted her to flirt with Zach? Fine, all right. Tonight was about his fantasies. She could do it. If he regretted it afterward, that was on him, not her.

Please don't regret it afterward.

She'd had only one drink, and then a glass of water, so her legs were steady as she made her way across the dance floor to slide onto the barstool next to Zach.

Zach took a moment to place her, and then his whole face lit up. He was beautiful when he smiled, beautiful no matter what. The desire bubbling up inside her felt dangerous, like playing with fire, but if Sam wanted to see her indulge, she would indulge. "Abby!" He leaned in to give her a hug, a bit awkward across their barstools. "What the hell are you doing here? Where's your husband?" He looked around, his brow furrowing.

"He's over there on the couch." She gestured over to Sam, who raised a hand in greeting, looking casual as can be. "It's great to see you again."

"Same. You know, I thought once I moved back, I might be running into people I knew, but this is a much more pleasant surprise than I expected." Zach's eyes sparkled.

"I didn't know you knew how to salsa dance."

"I learned in Florida." Zach winked. "It's a great place to pick people up."

The song changed, a pulsing beat mimicking her heart rate. "Do you want to dance?" she asked.

Zach paused, then looked over at Sam, who was still watching them with a placid expression on his face. "Your husband is cool with that?"

Oh, to tell him the truth. "Of course," she said, smiling. "You and I are old friends."

"Well, then." Zach slid off the stool and held out his

hand. "I suppose it couldn't hurt."

Apparently Zach was not worried about offending Sam. Now that he had her on the dance floor, he swept her up against him, holding her right against his warm body, and moved with her like they had been born to it. He was easy to follow, shifting with the beat, guiding her along. He'd be like this in bed. The thought slipped into her mind unbidden. People fucked the way they danced, and Zach danced with easy confidence and grace.

"You come here often?" he asked, and it was so much like a pickup line, she laughed.

"No, we haven't been here in years. What about you?"

"First time back since I moved. Seems like it's a night for coincidence." He smiled at her, white teeth flashing in the light, and suddenly a jolt of vibration raced up through her clit and made her breath catch in her throat. Zach didn't notice, spinning her around and pulling her back into his embrace. Abby caught Sam's eye over on the couch, and he was smiling wickedly, his phone in his lap. Holy shit. He lifted his chin, a bit of challenge, and the vibration turned up a whole additional level.

Only with extreme concentration could she keep her wits about her. Pressed up against Zach like this, if he moved his knee between her legs, shifted minutely to dance more intimately with her, he would feel the vibration. She couldn't let him know. She had to hide this spiraling pleasure, the buildup to climax that, if she was very careful to ignore, she could probably keep at bay.

"How come we never dated back in college, Abby?" Zach stepped back, giving a few respectful inches between them.

"We were never single at the same time?" Abby shifted her hips, rocking the vibrator against her while she kept time to the music. "Ahhh...um...and I didn't know if you were into me."

Zach laughed. "Come on. How could I not be? Look at you." He backed up, holding her at arm's length, eyeing her curves.

Abby blushed. But Sam had wanted her to flirt, and she wanted to flirt, so she spun around and looked at him over her shoulder. "How about this side?"

"Abby Wood If She Could." He pulled her back against him, crossing her own arms over her belly with his grip on her wrists. Every line of him pressed against her own softness. "You're teasing me something crazy."

His lips were only a centimeter from her ear. If she leaned one way, he could bite her earlobe, tease that sensitive spot, kiss her all the way down her neck. Fuck, she wanted this, and she shouldn't, shouldn't want anything like this. But then, the vibrator turned up all the way, a sudden spike of can't-escape pleasure racing up through her body. This was going to happen, with Zach's body pressed right against her back, his arms wrapped around her, Sam watching from the couch, and she bit her lip for silence as this pleasure built.

And then…it stopped. She wobbled, short of an orgasm, the desperation so fresh in her skin it burned. Oh, God, what was she doing? Did she really want to come here, in Zach's arms? She straightened, catching the rhythm of the dance again, regulating her breathing as her clit throbbed, unfulfilled.

"Easy there." Zach placed a kiss on her cheek, right on her jawbone, and spun her around to face him. Her arousal was ebbing back to something normal, the simmering desire beneath her skin, and the vibrator lay silent between her legs. She caught her breath. Zach was looking at her like he wanted to take her into his arms and kiss the breath right out of her once again.

Fuck, this was already going too far. She forced a smile as the music changed. "Thanks for the dance. I'm gonna go check in with Sam." She let go of his hands and wobbled on shaky legs over to the couch.

• • •

Sam could not wait to get his hands on Abby again. He'd known it would be hot to see her dance with someone else, just like it was hot imagining her with someone else in his fantasies. But he'd had the vibrator. He could tease her, and then do more than tease her. As he had watched, she'd pressed back against Zach, closed her eyes, her mouth falling open, and approached her orgasm…but he'd stopped her short. He could have taken her all the way. No one else would have been able to tell, but he didn't want that, not exactly like this.

He wanted more.

She came over to him and sat beside him on the couch, and he kissed her hard. She tasted like alcohol and sin and everything he wanted to devour. She shivered in his arms, soft, pliant, receptive. She'd been brought near the edge, and arousal must be burning her veins. She wasn't the only one: his cock was hard enough to burst the seams on his trousers. She brushed against him, her hand skimming up his thigh and then not so innocently touching his length, and he gasped against her mouth.

"You didn't let me come," she murmured.

"Did you want that?" he asked between kisses. "Want me to make you come in Zach's arms? Have him hold you as you fell apart?"

Abby moaned. "It sounds filthy like that."

"It is. It's filthy. Filthy for you to come while another man holds you." This was turning a corner in his mind, and he had to tell her what was really on his mind, had to confess this while he was still fuzzy from arousal and alcohol and the intoxicating taste of Abby. He broke the kiss and glanced at the bar, where Zach was now sitting on a barstool, watching him and Abby. What must be going through Zach's mind right now? Did he know?

"I don't want you to come while he's dancing with you. I want you to come while he's fucking you."

Abby's lips parted, her eyes going wide, then narrow, filled with lust. She licked her lips, pink tongue stroking over the sensitive petal-soft flesh, and oh, if only those lips were wrapped around his cock right now, or even better, wrapped around someone else's cock while he watched. She locked eyes with him. "Say it again."

The words spilled out, filthy and honest. "I want to watch you two together. I want to tell him how to fuck you and tell you how to please him. I want to see you come on his cock." He'd never given voice to these thoughts before, just like he'd never thought about power exchange, but everything entwined in his brain to watching Abby coming helplessly apart in climax.

Abby glanced over at the bar, indecision on her face.

"Do you want to fuck him?" Sam asked. This couldn't be a favor. This couldn't be something she did just for him. "Don't do this just to please me."

Abby's expression turned hesitant, then guilty. "I had a thing for him. Back in college. We never hooked up." Abby bit her lip, but she wasn't turned off by the idea; her flushed cheeks and rapid breathing told him all he needed to know. She wanted this, and maybe she didn't *want* to want it, but the signs were all over her face.

"It's okay," he said, more quietly, and she could probably read his lips more than hear him.

Abby got to her feet, then paused once more, and Sam nodded at her. Then she went over to the bar, crossing the dance floor without another look to either side, and moved into Zach's space, close enough to touch.

If only he could be a fly on the wall to hear what she said to him. But it wasn't much, maybe just an invitation to talk, before she took him by the hand and led him over to the couch where Sam was sitting.

Zach sat down on Abby's other side, a look of puzzled interest on his face, but not so much puzzlement as one might expect. Maybe he knew what was coming. Maybe he could read the signs.

Abby let go of his hand, put both hands on her thighs, and angled her body slightly toward Zach. He was a beautiful man, with his thick, curly hair and that tawny skin that was practically gold. Right now, his gaze flicked between Sam and Abby. Abby was the one who spoke. "Thanks for dancing with me earlier."

Zach laughed, a surprised laugh, and stretched one arm along the back of the couch. Like Abby, he angled his body, those long legs close to brushing hers. "It was not a favor, I promise. I would dance with you anytime." As if remembering Sam, he looked past Abby. "You're a lucky man, with a beautiful woman like this."

"Thanks." Sam could be the one to broach this, but it felt weird, like he was brokering some sort of exchange, and then Abby spoke up.

"You were wondering why we never hooked up in college," she said. "How we just kept missing each other. Ships in the night." With one tentative hand, she reached out and rested her fingertips on Zach's leg. All the air left the room, and Sam felt the touch on his own body, suddenly dizzy with the tension and unexpected intimacy. "What if we gave that another chance?"

Zach stilled. His gaze flickered from Abby to Sam, and back again. "I think you should be a little more specific."

Abby didn't look away. "Sam and I have been trying a few new things. And he"—she paused, taking a breath—"likes to watch."

Zach relaxed, that same lazy smile crossing his face. "Interesting." He turned his attention to Sam. "I can't say I blame you. Abby is gorgeous."

"I want to watch her with another man." Sam said it again, confessing this into the anonymous darkness of this club, confessing to this person, confessing it to himself. "I want to watch her with you. I want to see you make her come apart."

Zach stroked a thumb across his bottom lip, thinking, looking at them each in turn. "What about you, Abby?" His smile turned wicked, a lustful, playful smile. "Do you want me to fuck you?"

Abby shuddered, all the way down her body, and turned aside with a blush and a laugh, pulling her hand back from his leg. "God, Zach, just blurting it out like that."

"That wouldn't have bothered you ten years ago," Zach said. "Ten years ago, you'd have asked for what you want. So ask for what you want."

She turned to face Zach, but one of her hands went to Sam's knee, resting there, anchoring her to him even as she looked at the other man. "I want you to fuck me."

Zach lifted his arm from the back of the couch and slid it gently into Abby's red hair. Less than a foot from Sam's face, his fingers carded through those locks, cupping the back of her head, holding her. Abby's fingers dug into Sam's thigh, her grip tightening. Zach leaned in and closed his mouth over hers.

Jesus Christ. The secondhand sensation resonated through Sam's whole body like a caress, and Abby's hand gripping his thigh echoed her gasp. Zach kissed her like he had all the time in the world, and here, only inches away, Sam watched him coax her mouth and slant her head to the side.

Then, slowly, he pulled away. His hand slipped from

Abby's hair, the tresses falling back where they were, and he licked his lips as if to savor her taste. He turned to Sam first, and asked once more. "You want to watch me fuck your wife?"

The words stuck in Sam's throat, but from desire, not hesitation. "More than anything."

"Abby." Zach smiled at her, gently touching her cheek. "Do you want me?"

Abby exhaled. "Yes."

Zach licked his lips once more, then nodded. "Where do you live?"

Chapter Six

Abby's nerves were jangling by the time they got home. She'd driven, having had only one drink, and their car ride was pretty silent. Fortunately, so was the vibrator, a kickoff to the evening that was escalating faster than she intended.

"You sure about this?" she asked Sam again, for the first time since they'd said it in the club.

"Completely. You?" He glanced over at her.

"Yes." She swallowed. "I'm nervous."

"That's okay. You don't have to do anything you don't want to do."

That was such a glimpse of the Sam she was familiar with, the Sam who would never push her comfort zone even when she wanted to be pushed, and it simultaneously comforted and frustrated her. "I *do* want this. I want all of it."

She parked the car in front of their house, the lights from Zach's car swinging into the driveway behind them.

"You ever do this before?" Sam asked.

"Never." Nothing anything remotely like this. "This is a first."

"Good."

He leaned across the car and kissed her, hard, his mouth bruisingly intense. This was a claiming kiss, a kiss of certainty, a kiss that made her knees go weak. "Come on." He followed up that kiss with a light one. "Let's get inside."

Zach took his coat off at the door and accepted Sam's offer of a Scotch and soda, sitting next to Abby on the couch. He looked around, complimenting the house, the location close to town, the normal bits of small talk one would have with a new visitor. Outside of the dim lights and pounding music of the club, reality pressed in on all sides, and Abby still wanted this. They were sitting so close their knees brushed, and she took some of the whisky Sam offered in order to settle her nerves.

Sam sat down on the chair nearby, but not on the sofa with her and Zach. How did someone start something like this? There was a moment where he was in the house, welcomed, having a drink, having polite conversation, and somehow, this was supposed to move to the bedroom. Sometime. Anytime.

Zach's hand drifted to the back of Abby's neck again, where he'd touched her in the club, right before kissing her. He brushed his fingers lightly through her wavy hair, sending a shiver all the way down her body. Another pause, a moment where her body lit up from the inside. Zach stroked his fingertips lightly on the back of her neck. "Do you want to show me around?"

Abby got shakily to her feet, smoothing her dress down her hips. She put her mostly untouched whisky on the coffee table next to Zach's drink, then looked at Sam. This was a moment for him to say he needed more time, or wasn't ready, or something like that. Instead, he leaned back, crossed one ankle over his other knee, and sipped his whisky, his eyes dark with lust.

"Well." Sam smiled devilishly and gestured down the

hall. "You'd better go show him around."

There weren't many rooms to show in their small house, and all too soon they were in the bedroom, Abby's heart pounding as she flicked on the light. She turned to face Zach, ready to say something unnecessary about this being the bedroom.

He was closer than she had expected. When she breathed in, she could smell his cologne. Whatever words she was going to say vanished from her lips, and she froze, suddenly caught up in the weight of that moment.

Reaching up, Zach slid one hand into Abby's hair, cupping the back of her head while he stepped in the rest of the way. He pressed up against her, his whole body aligning with hers, and kissed her as confidently and thoroughly as he had in the club. His mouth slanted over hers, firm and hot, and every bone in her body went liquid. His arms around her were the only reason she didn't melt into the floor. With his hand in her hair like this, she felt completely enclosed, held, fully engulfed in this moment. She hadn't kissed another man in so long, not until tonight. It was the same and yet totally different from kissing Sam. And hotter. And illicit. Or maybe hot because of how illicit it was? It was hard to think, and then he had his tongue in her mouth, and fuck, Zachary Levine could *kiss*.

When he pulled away, she was dazed, and it took a minute for her brain to catch up to her body. She was standing in her bedroom with a man she was going to fuck, a man who was not her husband.

Right. Her husband. Sam. He'd somehow come in while she was kissing Zach, and she hadn't realized it, and now he was sitting in the chair in the corner, posed in the same way he'd been in the living room, ankle over knee, and he'd even brought the whisky with him. Watching. When she looked over at him, dazed, he smiled a small, intimate smile just for her, the kind that made a little shiver run down her spine. Zach looked over, too, an uncertain expression on his face, and Sam lifted his chin slightly in a nod.

Zach leaned in to kiss Abby again. She could get lost in those kisses, the way the sweep of his tongue drove the world away, his lips teasing her mind into nothingness. A sudden brush of fabric against her thighs made her break the kiss and look down. Zach was tugging at the hem of her dress, lifting it up. "I want to get you out of this."

She let him strip her, pulling that dress up and off, leaving her in front of him in her black lace bra and panties, the ones she'd put on earlier when Sam had first shown her the vibe. The vibe she was still wearing, that Zach would undoubtedly discover soon enough.

Zach let out a slow breath of air through pursed lips, almost a whistle but not quite, and then, "Damn." His eyes had settled on her breasts, straining the generous cups of her bra. He moved in again, but then paused. "I'll stop anytime. Just ask."

Abby huffed out a laugh. "Don't you dare stop."

In the corner, Sam chuckled, and the sound of his laugh was as reassuring as any words he could have spoken. Smiling, Zach cupped her breasts through her bra, his large hands warm against her skin, his touch sending a shiver through her body. A gentle squeeze, just a bit of pressure, and she was pressing herself farther into his grip. He brushed his thumbs over the nipples hardening inside the lace cups, the light touch making her tremble. He was watching her reactions this whole time. When he gave them a gentle twist, just a bit, she had to let out a little breath of air.

Nodding knowingly, he did it again, harder, evoking more of a moan. She couldn't help making noise.

To her surprise, Zach looked over at Sam and addressed him directly. "So she likes it rough like that?"

"She does." Sam raised his glass to his lips. "You can probably go harder."

Those words hit Abby like a physical touch, arousal spiking through her body. Zach's answering grin made Abby's toes curl, and the way he twisted her nipples even harder made her sag against his touch. He could make her come apart just like this, standing in the middle of her bedroom. But she didn't want to just be a passive recipient. She wanted to participate.

Zach let her unbutton his dress shirt and cast it aside, then pulled his undershirt over his head. His chest was muscled, the leanness of a swimmer's body plus the additional build from age, and the tone of his skin made him look like a gleaming golden statue in the soft light of the lamps. After a moment's hesitation, she put a hand flat on the center of his chest, the warmth from his skin radiating into hers.

"Come on." Zach took her wrist in his hand and stepped in closer to her. "How about you get on the bed?"

"Thought you'd never ask." She licked her lips and watched him follow her tongue, then he used that grip on her wrist to pull her closer for another fierce, harsh kiss. That one took a moment to recover from. Across the room, Sam was watching, and that made the situation more real, more exciting and dangerous, but also somehow...comforting. He would be here the whole time.

Abby sat down on the bed, scooting into the middle, as Zach climbed up onto it with her. There was another man in her bed. Someone who wasn't Sam, someone who wanted her, someone who was going to fuck her while her husband *watched* her get fucked. Jesus. It was amazing he couldn't see her heart beating through her chest.

He didn't ask before reaching behind her to find the clasp on her bra, and he removed it expertly, one-handed. She hadn't had a guy do that since high school. She was half naked, down to just her underwear, in front of this man she barely knew and hadn't seen since college, this man who was leaning in to kiss her like he meant it, this man who was pushing her down onto the bed and lying on top of her. He kissed his way down her neck, finding the place where it met her shoulder, and he bit down gently, then a little harder. "Hmm." He made a little happy noise and then moved farther down her body until he was hovering at her breasts, and he sucked one nipple into his mouth.

She swore and arched up off the bed. Her gaze found Sam still sitting on the chair, his whisky set aside now, watching her intently with lust in his eyes. Zach moved to her other breast, biting the nipple and pinching the one he had left. She was on fire, burning up from the inside out, and she was soaking wet through her underwear.

"I love how you squirm." Zach caught the edge of her underwear with his fingers, giving her a cheeky smile. "May I?"

Dazed with lust, she nodded. "There's…something," she began, but he was already pulling the scrap of fabric from her body, leaving her naked in front of him…naked except a small, teal vibrator nestled between her folds.

Zach stared down, puzzlement swiftly shifting to amusement. "Are you wearing a vibrator? Were you wearing a *vibrator* to the club tonight?" He looked over at Sam, then down at Abby, incredulous and amused.

Abby started laughing, because it was all so ridiculous and amazing, and nodded.

"Fuck, that is so hot." He dropped back down to kiss her again, fierce, firm, breathtaking. "Did you have it on when you were dancing with me?"

"I did," she confirmed.

"Jesus. If only I had known." He groaned, then dropped his head to her chest, as if it were all too much. Then he moved away from her to slip out of his slacks, revealing a substantial erection behind black boxer briefs. This couldn't be real. Sam was focused on them both, and having two sets of eyes watching was somehow *more* than twice as intense. Both of them made her feel beautiful.

"Can I remove this?" Zach asked, his finger resting against the vibrator, over her clit, so close to touching her directly. She nodded, suddenly struggling to find breath. He carefully, carefully slid the toy from her soaked pussy, his fingers barely brushing her as he did so. It came away glistening with her juices. Then, holy fucking shit, he *licked* it.

She made a noise, a choked gasp, and he grinned and did it again. "You taste incredible," he murmured, before putting the toy on the nightstand and kneeling between her legs. Before she could recover, he spoke to Sam. "Tell me how you want me to touch her."

Sam's answer came right away. "Spread her open. Don't let her hide."

The command in his voice was so damn hot. Zach sat cross-legged between her thighs, forcing her legs apart with his position. She was exposed like this, body lewdly stretched out for his perusal. He looked down at her pussy. "You're so wet. Look at you. You like having a strange man between your legs?"

Laughing, half embarrassed, she pulled her hands up to cover her face. Zach reached up and gently pulled her wrists away, making a noise of disapproval.

"No hiding. I want to watch your face when I do this." Eyes locked on hers, He dragged his fingers slowly through her wetness, rubbing across her swollen clit. The contact jolted her like touching a live wire, making her hips jerk. She wanted to close her legs and pull away, it was so intense and surprising. The second time, less surprising but no less intense, knife-sharp inside her senses. Zach rubbed her with two fingers, sliding the pads of his fingertips back and forth across her clit, pressing it in each direction and sparking her nerves with every pass. This wasn't just arousal running in her blood but something hotter, something fiercer, pleasure so crisp it bordered on pain.

Sam's voice from the corner jolted her as much as Zach's touch, especially the pairing of the two together, Sam's words overlaying Zach's actions so she could not forget they were both there. "Slide your fingers into her."

Abby looked to Sam again, past Zach, her gaze resting on his face. His lips were parted, eyes hooded, hands gripping the armrests of the chair. Yes, Sam was loving this, his expression drenched with lust.

When Zach slid two fingers smoothly all the way into her pussy, Abby's mouth opened with a wordless cry, her gaze still locked with Sam's. Her head fell back and her eyes closed as Zach fucked her with his fingers, curling them upward so every movement pressed her G-spot. Her muscles gripped at him, tightening reflexively with each pass, the pleasure beginning to build now.

"Abby."

She had closed her eyes, and opened them again at the sound of Sam's voice. He was still watching her, still intent. "Do you want him to fuck you?"

He had to know her answer, and they had of course already talked about this, but hearing the words right now felt different when she was desperate to come. She nodded, but Sam lifted his chin. "Ask him."

Abby looked up into Zach's face, staring into his eyes. How disorienting, how intimate and overwhelming to be rocking her hips against his hand while she stared into his eyes. "Will you fuck me? Please?"

Zach's eyes closed for a minute, and he drew his tongue across his bottom lip like he was trying to keep himself together as much as she was in this moment.

"God, yes." Slowly, he slid his fingers out of her pussy, dragging their tips along her G-spot again, sending a new shower of electricity through her nervous system. Still locked in her gaze, he put his fingers into his mouth and sucked them clean, and she might implode just from the look on his face.

Zach stripped off his boxer briefs, and suddenly he was naked. Right there. Another man, naked, in her bedroom, while she was also naked, and this was *real* and not one of her fantasies. Zach dug a condom out of the pocket of his jeans on the floor, actually taking out a whole strip of condoms still attached together. Abby laughed, making him look up in surprise. "You had high hopes for the club tonight?" she teased.

"It's good to be prepared, right?" Zach smiled, tearing one packet off the strip and tossing the rest onto the nightstand. "This is better than anything I'd hoped for, though." He slid the condom carefully down over his shaft, slicking it all the way to the base, giving his dick another stroke after it was on.

"How do you want me?" She looked from Zach to Sam and back again.

Zach stared at her naked body like he wanted to eat her alive, his expression enough to make her squirm. "I really want to fuck you from behind."

She and Sam seldom fucked like this, the position not one he usually enjoyed. It felt really different to be getting on all fours facing Sam instead of having him behind her. He was only a few feet away, and as she watched, he slowly unzipped his pants and took out his own cock. As Zach moved in behind her, nudging her legs apart with his, Sam began to stroke himself. Zach slid his fingers into her once more, this time from behind, the angle totally different, and she tightened up and sucked in a breath of air. It was hard to breathe, her body trembling with anticipation and nerves.

"Keep your eyes on me." Sam's voice made Abby jerk her head up, locking eyes with him again. And so, when Zach nudged her with the tip of his cock, she kept her eyes locked with Sam's while Zach pushed all the way into her. She moaned out loud as he stretched her open so good, bottoming out, his hips flush against her ass. His fingers trembled where they held her hips. Another man was inside her. She had another man's cock *inside* her.

"Fuck," Zach said behind her, his voice wrecked with emotion. "You're so tight. My God. Is she always this tight?"

"She is. I love loosening her up, getting her all wet and sloppy around me." Sam kept talking, this absolutely filthy shit, and Zach began to thrust in and out of Abby in long, slow strokes. "She makes these perfect noises."

Zach thrust hard, once, and Abby gasped, mouth falling open.

"Yeah. Just like that." Sam nodded. "Wait until you feel her come. She's gonna squeeze around you so good."

Abby bit her lip, whimpering, clenching up reflexively. She didn't know it would be this hot to have them talking about her like this, as if she wasn't here or couldn't answer. Zach gripped her hanging breasts, squeezing them with each stroke. This position was like being trapped, like she had to just kneel here and take it, and that was hitting a whole bunch of her kinks. She wanted him to keep pounding into her, his cock spreading her folds, his balls brushing her with each thrust. When he pinched her nipples, rolling them hard between his fingers, she yelped and squeezed down around him.

Zach groaned, then squeezed her nipples one more time, creating the same response. She couldn't help it; it was like a direct connection from her nipples to her clit. When she squirmed, his cock moved inside her, reminding her where she was, what was happening, what she was doing. He let go of her nipples and switched to her clit, balancing himself with a hand on her back while he reached below her and rubbed that small, tight bud.

"Oh God. I can't..." Her body was trembling, her arms starting to give out from the intensity of it all. She collapsed down onto her forearms and managed to just lift her head. Sam was still watching her, breathing fast, rubbing his cock with firm, easy strokes. The climax built, curling up through her toes and her legs and her pussy, gathering like a heavy weight. Words slipped through her mind as fast as she could think them, unable to hold onto them, a steady stream of curses and words of pleasure. Her body was like a tuning fork struck, humming all one note of *God, yes, this,* tightening up impossibly into a coil of energy ready to explode.

Her orgasm tore through her body, shattering her with fierce pleasure, and she couldn't watch Sam anymore, couldn't keep her head up, just collapsed onto her folded arms and shook and clenched over and over around Zach's hard cock. He was swearing, moving in short, tight thrusts, so fast it was like a blur of friction, chasing his own pleasure. As her climax began to ebb, he let go of her clit and gripped her hips with both hands, driving in deep and full and finally all the way, cock pumping with his own orgasm.

In the moments that followed, she rested in silence. Her breathing, the slight twitches of Zach's hands on her hips, the sudden quiet in the room...it all combined into a single soundscape of peaceful aftermath. Zach pulled out, slowly sliding from her warmth, and the bed dipped as he shifted away. Abby curled over onto her side, resting, her hair tumbling across her face.

A gentle hand on her shoulder made her jump. She opened her eyes, and Sam was there, brushing her hair back. He'd dressed himself again, tucking his cock away, and she could see the line of it straining his pants.

The bed dipped again. Abby sat up, looking between the two men. Sam raised his eyebrows. "You okay?"

A blush heated her cheeks, and damn, how the hell could she blush right now, after all this?

"I'm good." She grinned that lazy post-sex grin and looked over at Zach, who had pulled his boxer briefs on and was now clearly trying to gauge the emotion in the room. "You good?"

"Fuck, yeah, I'm good." He laughed. Then, sitting back on the bed, he looked between the two of them. "Sam, are you all right? I don't think I could watch that without coming all over the place."

"I got close, but not quite." He smiled and shifted his erection in his pants. "It's...okay."

Zach rubbed his jaw. "I might be overstepping here. But...you ever have somebody else watch you two fuck?"

Abby and Sam looked at each other. "Not yet."

Zach grinned. "Do you want to?"

• • •

Having Zach sit in the chair was something totally different. Sam was already amped up from what had just happened, from watching Abby come like a wild animal while Zach fucked her, and it was so God damned hot that he wasn't sure he was going to recover. Besides that, he was going to be fantasizing about this for a long time to come. So now, with Zach just casually throwing out there that he wanted to watch, Sam was tossed into this entirely different perspective on the whole thing that was nonetheless hot as fuck, just in a different way.

Zach slipped his pants back on and sat back down again, this time in the same armchair Sam had just vacated. Sam was already pulling off his clothes, not even bothered by Zach's presence. Abby was soft and pliant in his arms, already less tense because of her orgasm. He was going to fuck her after another man had fucked her, and the prospect had his cock straining.

"How do you want me?" Abby blinked up at Sam, lazy and slow. Sam thought about it for just a moment.

"Ride me."

He lay sideways on the bed, perpendicular to how they slept, angling himself deliberately so Zach could watch. They were already into this, so might as well go all the way. His legs draped off the edge of the bed, and his eyes were only on Abby as she straddled him. She looked down at him, and her body was still so soft and warm, so freshly fucked, that glow about her making her even more appealing.

Abby moved to kneel next to him, and after another quick glance at Zach, she bent suddenly and took Sam's cock into her mouth. *Fuck.* Her mouth was hot and wet, and she swallowed him down without any hesitation. After stroking himself watching her and Zach, this was too much stimulation, an overwhelming rush of pleasure into his senses. "Holy shit," he breathed, and his hands went to her head automatically, tangling in her hair, wanting and needing to feel her right here. He didn't force her head down or try to control her speed or depth at all, just needed the solidity of touching her. Already, his balls were tightening, his body begging for release. He had to tell her to stop before he really wanted to. He didn't want to come like this.

Abby swept her long red hair back and licked her lips, and damn, she looked so fucking *smug.*

"Are you trying to kill me?" he asked, laughing and gasping.

"Maybe." She winked, then straddled his hips and positioned herself over him. Her breasts hung tantalizingly close, so he had to reach up and squeeze them. Zach's hands and mouth had just been on these. He rolled her nipples between his fingers harder than he normally would, just to feel her twitch and moan, then even harder, making her gasp and bite her lip.

"Too much?" he asked.

She shook her head. "I like it."

Gripping her hips, he eased her down all the way onto his cock.

As he slid into her, Sam watched Abby's eyelids fall half closed and her mouth fall open. She was slick around his cock, completely soaking wet, her pussy so easy to penetrate. The thought of fucking her right after someone else was just as hot as the sex. He used her hips for leverage as he thrust up, arching into her, angling each thrust exactly how he knew she liked. God, she was beautiful. She had her eyes closed now, her head tipped back, biting her lower lip, hotter than the hottest porn he had ever watched.

"Look at Zach."

At the sound of his voice, Abby opened her eyes, blinking, still rocking her hips against him with all the instincts she had driving her forward. She seemed to take a moment to process, and then lifted her chin to look up and over at Zach, who was sitting in the chair watching them intently. Immediately, she let out a little whimper.

"He's watching you. He's watching me fuck you. Do you like that?"

Without looking away from Zach, Abby nodded. She had started giving these little hitching breaths with every stroke. Thrusting a hand between her legs, she began to rub her clit, fingers moving back and forth across her bud. God, he was going to come, he was going to fucking *explode,* and he twisted her nipples again as she tightened up and crashed over the edge into orgasm.

That first long, hard squeeze finally, finally sent him over the edge. Instead of everything vanishing, the way the world sometimes did in orgasm, everything became amplified. Every sensation crystallized: Abby's pussy squeezing his dick, her desperate cries, the weight of Zach's gaze from the corner, the escalating waves of climax running through his own body, everything that had led to this moment culminating like a never-ending breathless eternity.

"Fucking hell." Sam threw an arm over his head as he caught his breath. They were all still for a few heartbeats, pausing to come down, and then Abby slid off him. After cleaning up, he pulled his boxers back on while Abby wrapped herself in a robe. Zach got up from the chair and, to Sam's pleased surprise, walked up to Abby, wrapped his arms around her, and kissed her. It wasn't the passionate, lust-filled kisses of before, the ones where he looked like he was trying to take down all her defenses at once. This was sweet and compassionate and warm, and he stepped back afterward to look over at Sam with a relaxed smile. "Is it too late to finish that drink?"

Chapter Seven

"And then he just, what? Went home?" Angela interrupted herself to lift one of the dresses off the rack, a long beaded piece. "What about this one?"

"Too beaded." Abby moved over to another rack, this one full of long, flowing pieces, and began sorting through them. "He left after his drink. And that was it. Sent me and Sam a message when he got home, thanking us for a fun night, and asking us to call him anytime."

"Holy shit." Angela stepped away from the rack where she'd been searching. "And what happened when he left?"

"We just...hung out." Abby shrugged. "It was casual. Sam made me a cup of tea, and we cuddled on the couch, kind of like we used to. Which was weird, now that I think about it, since we haven't done that kind of thing in a while."

"What, cuddle?"

"Yeah. Just cuddle and hang out." She picked up a long black dress and held it up. This would highlight her curves pretty well, especially with that deep V-neck. She wanted to dress to impress for Sam's company party, since this was the first party since he'd been promoted, and she had a soft spot for dress shopping, especially with these after-holiday sales still lingering into the end of January. Her thoughts kept returning to the other night, though, her time with Zach and with Sam, the dreamlike quality of it all.

The dressing room was empty, nobody else shopping for dresses at this hour on a weeknight, and she and Angela had privacy to keep talking as Abby went into a dressing room to try on a few final contenders.

"I'm worried," Abby came out with at last, trying to put words to the collection of feelings swishing around inside her. "We keep one-upping everything. We started with these fantasies, and now it's escalating every time. I don't even know what's going to be next. It's technically my turn, but I feel weird to bring anything up at all."

Angela's voice came from the other side of the door. "What are you thinking about bringing up?"

"I don't know." The problem wasn't really coming up with a new fantasy. It's just that *this* particular fantasy had unlocked a whole bunch of dormant feelings inside her, feelings she'd managed to keep tamped down since first meeting Sam.

"Well, are you both into it so far?"

Abby paused in front of the mirror in her underwear and bra, holding the dress in both hands, mind suddenly filled with the memory of Sam's expression as Zach brought her to climax. She had to swallow to clear the knot of emotion in her throat. She could probably get off to just that mental image. "We're both into it." Shit, they were *more* than into it. She'd never seen Sam act like this before. "I'm…kind of worried about where we're headed with it."

"You said you didn't know what your next fantasy even is. Maybe there's nothing to be worried about."

Abby slid the dress over her head and smoothed it down, adjusting all the folds of fabric that had gotten caught on her curves, and looked at herself in the mirror. This was a great dress. She'd known it from the minute she'd held it on the rack, and on her body, it was even better. This was a sinful dress, the kind to make Sam stop and stare.

The kind to make everybody stop and stare. Stare, and flirt, and maybe more...

Ah, shit. She shouldn't want that, shouldn't even think about that. "Angela, do you think I'm a bad person?"

No answer came from the other side of the door. It wasn't like Angela to wander away while they were shopping, not without telling Abby first, so she was probably thinking about the weird-ass question Abby had just asked.

"Is this about you buying another dress while you already have, like, five of them in the closet?"

Abby rolled her eyes, which of course Angela couldn't see. "No." She opened the door of the dressing room. "What do you think?"

"About the dress, or you being a bad person?"

"About the dress."

Angela nodded. "It's hot. Buy it."

Abby checked herself out in the angled mirrors, looking at the dress from all sides. "I don't usually wear long dresses. It feels elegant."

"It's sexy as hell."

"Thanks."

"Now what's this about you being a bad person?"

Abby sighed, staring into her own eyes in her reflection, eyes that stared back at her, eyes that knew all the terrible things she was thinking. "Maybe we made a mistake taking Zach home with us."

Angela leaned against the wall next to the mirrors. "What do you mean? You were just saying you both had a great time."

"I know. We did. But..." To explain this was going to admit to some shit that gave her pause, even around Angela, who was never going to judge her for the wacky shit she thought or said. "Ever since we did it, I cannot stop thinking about fucking other guys."

Angela's eyebrows went up, but then she lowered them, returning to a normal expression. Abby pressed on. "It's not like I'd go off and do anything like that, but I keep thinking about it, like, it's on my mind all the time. I feel like my hormones have been turned up to eleven all week."

"That's probably normal, though. You just did this big thing. It was exciting. Your body wants more. It'll pass, if you just ignore it."

Abby grimaced. "I don't know. I feel really guilty about it. I chose Sam, my one and only. I shouldn't be thinking about other guys."

Angela waved a hand dismissively. "Fantasies are just fantasies. They don't mean anything. You don't have to act on them."

Except that they were kind of doing that, bringing up fantasies and acting on them. Abby turned away from her own judgmental reflection and ducked back into the dressing room to take the dress off. "I'm worried that if we keep sharing fantasies, I'm just going to tell him. And then he'll be hurt, and we're never going to repair that."

"Maybe he won't be hurt. Maybe he'll be into it. He's been into everything so far."

"That's *worse*." She'd definitely already considered that possibility, too. "If he's into it, then we have this huge tectonic shift in our marriage. We go from just the two of us to... I don't know, just *past* the two of us, where I sleep with other people, and then we can never get anything back." She hung the dress on its hanger and pulled her jeans back over her hips. "Even in the last month, things have changed between us. They don't feel like they used to."

"In a good way or a bad way?"

Abby hesitated. "I don't know. Just different. Sam's different. He's not the same guy I married. It's like there's this whole other side of him that I hadn't known, just hanging out there, waiting for kinky sex games."

"But you like that side of him."

Angela had her there. "Yeah, I do. But—"

"But nothing. You can't have it both ways. You're having super-hot sex and making each other's fantasies come true. I don't get why you're upset about that."

Abby closed her eyes, sitting for a moment on the bench in the dressing room. Alone in that space, the guilt welled up inside her, another wave of discomfort. "This feels like old me. Irresponsible me. I'm not supposed to be attracted to other guys anymore."

"That's bullshit, you know. You're married, not dead."

"That's easy for you to say. I don't want to hurt Sam."

"I seriously think you're underestimating him."

What if she was wrong, though? Angela could speak confidently from out there; this was all a hypothetical exercise for her. It wasn't her life.

Abby looked down at her hands in her lap. "I worked so hard to change the train wreck I was becoming back in college, and I got a great guy like Sam out of it. I don't want to undo that."

Another long silence, then Angela's voice from right outside the door. "Are you still getting dressed in there, or are you sitting there feeling sorry for yourself?"

Abby wrinkled her nose and got up. "I'm coming, I'm coming."

After Abby bought the dress, they grabbed a soft pretzel at one of the mall kiosks and sat on a bench near Target, sharing it and people watching. They talked about Angela's bathroom remodel and several stories about her dog Thumper before circling back to the previous topic, which Angela brought up out of nowhere. "So do you want to go back to the way things were with you and Sam?"

Abby reeled from the subject change for a minute before recovering. "I don't think we could. And I kind of don't want to. I just don't want it to escalate. I don't want it to get out of control. And I definitely don't want him to know that I'm lusting after every good-looking guy in the vicinity."

Angela laughed, picking up a piece of pretzel. "I think it's okay. I actually think you should bring it up. See if that threesome was a one-and-done thing, or if he'd be game for it all over again."

Abby winced. "I don't know. Zach was kind of a special case. I don't think he'd be into making a habit out of it."

Angela shrugged. "You suit yourself. It's your marriage. You probably don't want my marriage advice, anyway. I'm never getting married again."

"Straight pimpin' with Angela?" Abby grinned.

"That sounds like a new HGTV show." Angela nicked the last of the pretzel and popped it in her mouth before Abby could object.

Maybe she should call it off. They might be having fun now, but they couldn't keep this up forever. There was a reason Abby Wood If She Could stayed behind at college: giving in to all her baser impulses was an unsustainable way to live. Relationships required people to grow up. This dalliance between them was destined to set them both up for bad expectations.

Even if the thought of calling it off made her feel just a little bit sick.

• • •

It figured that Abby could somehow find a dress even more sinfully gorgeous than her reunion dress to wear to this company party. That green dress from New Year's had been smokin' hot, but this was sex in fabric form, clinging to all her curves with a neckline plunging dangerously low.

Sam came up behind her as she finished curling her hair and set down the curling iron on the sink. She yielded to his touch, and he wrapped his arms around her and breathed in the floral scent of her red curls. "Maybe we should just skip the party so I can get you back out of that dress again."

"It's the company party and we have to go." She gently pulled away from his embrace. Her expression had been a little frowny, a little unhappy, all afternoon.

"You don't look like you want to go, I've gotta say." He tried to laugh a little so she wouldn't get her feelings hurt.

"Oh. Sorry." She shook her head. "I just... I had a chat with Angela a couple of days ago, and it's been on my mind."

He sat down on the bed. A chat with Angela could be anything. "You want to talk about it?"

Abby hesitated, a few emotions playing across her face. The longer she waited, the faster Sam's heart beat, as if they were in some sort of race of escalating emotions. Finally, she sighed, defusing all the tension, and walked out of the bathroom. "This thing we're doing just doesn't seem sustainable."

"What thing?" He had a sense, obviously, but hopefully he was wrong.

"This..." She waved her hand in a rolling motion. "This fantasy thing. Where we share fantasies and make them come true. We can't keep going like this."

"Why not?" They'd been having a good time, right? Last weekend with Zach was incredible, and all week, they had been chill together, no sense of distress. "It's been working out so far."

"But where's it gonna go?" She spread her arms wide, then leaned back against the doorframe of the bathroom. "We're just going to keep trying new things, week after week, forever?"

"I assumed we'd run out of fantasies, eventually." His

attempt at a joke didn't make her smile. She seemed really upset about this, or maybe…disappointed? Her expression was nearly neutral, hard to read, with a slight downturn of her lips. "But really." Sam got to his feet and approached, slowly, cautiously. "I thought we were having a good time. We haven't done anything the other person hasn't wanted to do."

"That's just it." She brushed through his arms and past him. "We're both into all this, but it's been only a month and we've been to a sex club, tried BDSM, and I fucked another guy!" She pressed a palm to her head, looking suddenly a lot more upset.

"Is that what this is about? Are you feeling guilty?" He really wanted to hold her right now, but she'd pushed away. Instead, he thrust his hands in the pockets of his suit pants. "Don't feel guilty, sweetie. I wanted it. I thought you wanted it. We had fun."

"And what about when you want to do it again?"

"We don't have to do anything we're not both into." How many times were they going to go through this? "Seriously, if you want to stop, we can stop, but I thought we were both having a good time. Eventually we'll either run out of fantasies or we'll get to a point where the other person doesn't want to participate. Otherwise, we're only doing stuff we're both into." He paused, a terrible thought running through his head. "Unless you're not into this? Unless you're saying yes because of some other reason?" Would she do that? Would she say yes when she meant no, just out of some desire to…to what?

"No." Her guilty expression shifted to angst, her eyes going wide. "No. I haven't been lying. I've been into all of this. I just feel like we can't go on forever."

"So let's not go on forever. Let's just go as long as we want." He wanted her to be okay with what they'd done. Even if she didn't want to ever do anything else, they couldn't close these doors on what had happened. He didn't want to. Sam moved closer again, and this time she let him take her hands. "Listen. Last weekend with Zach, it was huge. It was the hottest thing I've ever seen. Watching you with him... I've never been so turned on in my *life,* Abby, you have to believe that." She looked up at him, her eyes pleading, like she wanted this to be true, and he kept talking. "If you don't want to do anything else, if you really want to stop now, we can stop. You don't have to share any of your other fantasies. You already made mine come true. We don't have to do any of it again if you don't want to."

Abby's expression twisted, like she was trying to hide a range of emotions, and she settled on something neutral, something passive, frustratingly passive. "We're going to be late for the party."

"Then let's be late." They couldn't leave unless they resolved this. He wouldn't be able to sleep. "What do you want? Do you want to go back to how things were before all this?"

"We can't, and you know that." She pulled back, dropping her arms. "You know all these things about me now. You know I like getting teased, and tied up, and I like you to top me. You know I like being watched." Her face was growing pinker, slowly turning to red. "And I *liked* last weekend. I liked getting fucked by Zach. And I don't know how I'm supposed to feel about that. I shouldn't like that. I shouldn't be so *okay* with that. You're my husband, and you're supposed to be the only person I'm with."

Was that at the root of this? "I don't know how to convince you I'm okay with it."

She let out a long, shaky breath. "I guess I'm just having trouble with what it means for us, long-term. Who we are, you and me, as a couple." She looked off toward the window, folding her arms, her gaze going soft like she was lost in thought. "I'm okay," she said after a couple of moments. "I'm okay."

"You believe me, though, right?" She couldn't go thinking he was secretly resenting her for being attracted to

Zach. He needed confirmation, or all of this felt groundless. "You believe I liked last weekend, that I like all of it?"

She smiled at him, still something guarded about her smile. "I do believe you, yeah. I believe you had a good time last weekend. I believe that you are fine with everything." She looked like she was going to say something more, her lips opening once again, but then she closed them and didn't elaborate.

"Okay." He had to trust her; she was his wife. He had to trust that she would tell him the truth about these feelings.

She gestured for the door, shutting down the conversation. "Come on. You want to drive, or should I?"

• • •

Maybe this party was a bad idea.

Abby tipped back her glass of champagne and took another look around the Dooney Architecture Annual Gala. There was no denying it: Sam worked with a lot of hot guys. She'd always been aware of it on a distant level, but fresh off their new sexual adventures, her aesthetic interest had shifted into a lustier note.

Fuck.

The party wasn't huge, despite being called a gala; Dooney Architecture was a medium-sized firm, but they invited their interior design partner company, and with spouses attending as well, all in all there were probably about a hundred people here. Enough to see everyone but not enough to disappear completely. Abby wasn't normally the type to even *want* to disappear completely, but she couldn't figure out how she was supposed to act. Could she flirt? She flirted with everybody, but it was different to flirt when her interest was hypothetical versus when she was actually thinking about fucking someone.

"You all right?" Sam asked, touching the middle of her back and steering her over toward a waiter with passed appetizers. "You froze up for a minute, there."

Sam was gorgeous, no doubt about it. Looked good, smelled good, embodied everything she wanted in a man. Why was she even looking at anyone else?

"Just got lost in thought." She smiled up at him so he wouldn't see that she was a horny, guilty little mess. "Are those beef Wellington canapés?" She snatched one up and popped it into her mouth, just to have something to do.

"Sam and Abby!"

The deep, warm voice knocked her out of her daze as Stephan, one of the other architects Sam worked with, came over to greet them. He shook Sam's hand before pulling him into a hug, and then embraced Abby as well. God, *Stephan*. Tall, Greek, gorgeous, with curly black hair and dark eyes, this olive-skinned beauty had been a subject of Abby's admiration for, what, a year and a half now? Ever since she first saw him at the company's Labor Day picnic. Of course he would come over now, while she was a bundle of unsettled hormones, looking beautiful and enticing as ever. He even pronounced his name the gorgeous way, accent on the second syllable, as European as his heritage.

"It's nice to see you, Stephan," Sam said. "Jo join you tonight?"

Abby had only met Stephan's equally beautiful wife once, at that first Labor Day picnic.

"Jo's around here somewhere." Stephan glanced around. "Schmoozing, as usual." He laughed, warm and deep, and snagged a canapé from a passing waiter. "Are you having fun tonight? Abby, enjoying yourself?"

"Yes." Her mouth had dried up, and she didn't even say "thank you" or ask him how he was doing. That was an invitation to follow up with some other conversation, but no words came. Sam looked at her curiously. It wasn't like her to run out of small talk; these casual exchanges were her specialty.

Stephan seemed to be waiting for something else, but shifted the conversation smoothly. "I swear, these get more extravagant every year. I keep waiting for the invitation to say 'black tie,' and I won't be surprised."

"Tuxes are good," Abby blurted out. They both looked at her. Tuxes are good? Really? That was her meaningful addition to this conversation? "I mean. I like them. They look good. On people." Jesus, Abby, stop talking now. She was sounding like a blithering idiot.

Sam's eyebrows were both twitching upward, and he had that look that he was trying not to call her out on being a dumbass. He never would, not in public. "You want to see me in a tux?" he teased, smiling, defusing some of the tension.

"Yeah. Of course." She leaned in closer to him, closing some of the distance. Anything to space her farther away from Stephan, who was exuding some serious pheromones, or maybe she was just extra neurotic today.

Fortunately, Jo stepped up alongside Stephan and reached out a hand to Abby and Sam in greeting. Jo was as beautiful as Stephan, with short black hair cut in a pixie cut and dark eyes that could see right through you. Thank God people couldn't read minds, because Abby's thoughts had been nonstop filthy about Jo's husband.

"You working the room, hon?" Stephan looked down at his wife.

"You know me." She returned his warm smile. "It's been forever since I've seen you both. I keep being booked during all the seasonal parties. I have to let Stephan off loose on his own without a chaperone." Her gaze, staring back up at him, was filled with pure affection. "And who knows what kind of mischief he's been getting up to?"

"I'm always in trouble, honey, you know me." Stephan kissed the top of her head. "You can see I've already picked out a beautiful woman to talk to while you were absent. Sam is barely keeping me at bay."

He was kidding, obviously, but Abby flushed as Jo chuckled. "Ignore him, Abby, he's terrible." Jo reached out to squeeze Abby's hand.

Abby, still blushing, shook her head. "It's fine. He's fine. I mean, I don't mind. I don't mind his comments. Or anybody's comments." Shit, she was making this worse. "Hey, honey, I'm going to…go grab a drink at the bar." She ducked away from the conversation and headed straight for the bar.

He's fine? I don't mind anybody's comments? Escape was the only option. If only she could stop picturing Stephan pinning her against the wall with his tall, athletic body, holding both hands up above her head with just one of his, his mouth teasing slow, lazy kisses down her neck while she wriggled helplessly against him…

"Abby?"

She turned to see Sam, eyebrows drawn together in puzzlement. "Are you okay?"

"I'm fine. I was just getting a drink." Oh, but she wasn't standing at the bar yet. She was near the bar, but she hadn't approached it, instead staring into space on her own.

Sam was clearly not buying it. "Hey, babe, why don't we duck off somewhere quiet and talk?" He took her by the hand, his grip insistent, almost too tight. "Right now."

She let him pull her around the corner into the hallway leading to other parts of the banquet space, and then into a closet. He turned on a light. They were surrounded by shelves of holiday decorations. "What is up with you?" he asked. "You've been weird all night. Is this about what we talked about earlier? Are you mad at me or something?"

Ah, God, this was humiliating. "I'm not mad at you." She

put a hand to her head, like that might keep her emotions from welling up. Sam was a good guy. He didn't deserve to be lied to, and he didn't deserve the runaround she was giving him. "Look. I haven't been honest with you."

He stared at her, waiting, his whole body tense as he visibly braced for whatever she was going to say.

"I didn't have a problem sleeping with Zach last weekend because I had a thing for him. But it's not just him. I find a ton of guys attractive. You, obviously. I am *so* hot for you. But not just you. Other guys." She let out a breath. Sam wasn't talking yet, his expression still cautious, and she had to get all this out. "I slept with a lot of guys back in college, and you know that, and I'm not ashamed of that. I'm not. I know that's nothing to be ashamed of." Shit, this was way harder than she thought. "But that was old Abby. And I *am* embarrassed about her, me, who I used to be. Irresponsible, only caring about myself." Her eyes prickled hotly with tears, and she blinked them back, because she was *not* going to cry. She took a shaky breath and kept going. "I don't talk about college because I was a royal fuckup back then, and it almost ruined me. I was *this close* to flunking out, so, I decided to turn things around, and I left all that stuff behind. The dating around, the partying, the Campus Twenty. And then I found you. And you thought…you thought I was so wonderful, and I wanted to be wonderful for you. And I made a promise to you that I was going to be with you forever. You and only you. And I meant that. And now that we're doing all these things, these dares, I'm seeing this other part of myself come back, and I'm…" She closed her eyes. "I'm ashamed of her."

She took a minute to catch her breath before opening her eyes. Sam went to speak, but she held up a hand. "No wait. Let me finish. I shouldn't be that person anymore. I should have grown up. I should have become more mature. And now, I'm here in this party, and I'm looking around at all these guys, and I'm thinking about..." Shit, she might as well make this as bad as it could get. "I'm thinking about them fucking me. I'm having these fantasies that I just should *not* be having, and I'm embarrassed, and I feel like it's all started because we opened the floodgates with Zach, and we opened things up a little, and I don't know how to close them again." She twisted her hands together, thumbs pressing into the skin, the sensation some way to anchor herself and keep from flying apart. "I love you, and I don't want to lose you. And I'm sorry."

She braced herself for his response, whatever that might be.

• • •

Abby had to be kidding. There had to be another part of this story, the one where her literal freak-out made some sense. But that was it: she was still attracted to other men, and apparently, feeling really guilty about it.

"I don't understand."

She looked away. "I know. I know you're probably disappointed in me, and you might be a little disgusted. I know it was hot when it was Zach, but that was a one-time thing, a fantasy. I don't plan to act on any of these feelings, obviously. But I don't want you to be disappointed in me."

"No, I mean, I don't understand why you think I'd be upset by this."

"Because I'm turned on by other men!" she said. "Like Stephan! I think he's gorgeous, okay?"

"He *is* gorgeous—" Sam began, but Abby cut him off.

"Yeah, and I keep thinking about him, like, pushing me up against the wall and fucking me. Putting his hands all over me." She seemed to realize she was getting loud, and she clapped a hand over her mouth, and glanced toward the closet door. Outside in the hallway, everything was silent, and she continued a little quieter. "I don't want to cheat on you, Sam. I don't want you to think I ever would. I feel so fucking guilty about all of this. And it's all because of this game, because of this *stupid* game, and I'm having these feelings that I've been able to hide for years, and I can't hide them anymore."

Oh, Abby. He wanted so badly to touch her, and he started with her hands, gently closing her twisting fingers in his to try to settle them. "Abby, if I didn't want you to sleep with someone else, would you do it anyway?"

"Of course not, that's what I mean. I would never do anything to betray you." She was starting to get worked up, her voice catching.

"What if." He cupped her hands from both sides, holding hers gently. "What if I wanted you to sleep with someone else? Like with Zach. What if I wanted that again?"

Abby's face twisted in a confused grimace. "I don't know why you'd want that."

"Because it's fucking *hot,* Goddamn it." He pulled her closer to him. "I'm not ashamed of your past, and I don't want you to be, either. You don't have to change who you are for me."

"It's all mixed up in my head, though. Being a selfish, irresponsible college kid and...all this kinky stuff. They're from the same parts of my life. I worked hard to grow up." She looked down at their entwined hands. "And growing up meant I got a degree, a good job, and most of all, I got you. These fantasies make me feel like I'm betraying this person I worked hard to become."

She was really living with this kind of angst, this turmoil? "Abby. I would have loved you no matter what. I love you more than anything, can't you see that?" He squeezed her hands. "These fantasies don't mean anything. They certainly don't mean we don't love each other. They don't mean you aren't a talented, capable, responsible, gorgeous, *amazing* woman. Because you're all those things. And it is the fucking hottest thing in the entire world for me to watch you be that gorgeous, amazing woman you are with another man."

The color rose high on Abby's cheeks, a deep red flush. "I don't..." she began, but then trailed off.

"I love that you have these cravings. These urges. I love this side of you."

She was breathing more quickly, now, hope and worry and lust warring in her expression.

"I want to know you're being pleasured." He stepped into her, pushing her against the closed door of the closet, her tiny intake of breath so sweet in his ears. "I want to know that some other man is making you fall apart, that he's enjoying you as much as I do." He skimmed his hands down her sides, settling on her hips, and pulled her against him. At the press of his rigid erection against her soft belly, her eyes went wide and her mouth slack. "Does this convince you enough?"

Her eyelids fluttered. "But...I'm going to keep feeling this way. Aren't you worried?"

"Should I be?"

She bit her lip. "I would never do anything to hurt you, even if I wanted to. I don't want to want to."

"But I want you to want to." He smiled at how silly it sounded. "And I want you to want to want to."

Abby smiled as well, shaking her head. "This is ridiculous."

"Is it?"

He couldn't wait anymore; he had to kiss her, mouth hot and wet against hers. She moaned, soft, needy, and kissed him back. He kept speaking against her mouth, words spilling out. "I want to watch other men fuck you, Abby. Or not even watch. Maybe I want you to go meet some man and sleep with him, and come home and tell me about it. Give me all the sweet details while I slide in your tight, wet cunt."

"Oh God, Sam," she breathed, shuddering.

He had to get inside her, right now. He skimmed her dress up her hips, pushing her back against the door, which rattled. They both paused, and without another word, shifted so she was pressed against the wall beside the door instead. She helped, sliding her underwear off, letting them fall to the floor, and he was already fumbling with his trousers to push them down to his knees.

Abby lifted up on her toes, and he hiked one of her legs up over his hip and drove his length all the way inside her. She was drenched, hot and so snug around him. Her breath caught as he fucked into her, and she clawed at his shirt, her fingernails digging into his back.

"You like that?" he asked, voice deep like a growl. "You like the thought of me fucking your sweet, sloppy pussy after somebody else has already loosened you up?"

"Holy fuck, Sam." She shifted against him. "Yes, God, I love that."

"You want to fuck Stephan? Hmm? You like to think about his big cock splitting you open?"

"Shh, not so loud." She put a hand over his mouth, but he pulled away and whispered the next words into her ear.

"I love it. I love thinking about you like that. I want you to be a total slut for me."

She whimpered, her words trailing off, and that was just as well, because he could barely keep quiet himself. She squeezed around him like a tight, wet fist. "I can't..." she breathed, barely audibly. "You feel so big like this."

Her muscles were squeezing around him, so he must be stretching her, the position standing here tightening everything up for both of them. Items on the shelves near them were rocking with each thrust, their fucking less silent than when they'd started, but right now, Sam could only focus on this pleasure building deep inside his body. His climax was gathering from the soles of his feet, from every nerve ending. He couldn't touch her clit like this, one of his arms bracing himself above her head, the other keeping her knee hiked up over his hip. He wanted her to come. Wanted to see her face when she couldn't hold it in anymore, wanted that blissful expression to wash over her, that viselike grip as she clenched over and over again in pleasure.

Her breath stuttered, fingernails suddenly biting into his skin though the fabric of his shirt, and her whole body seized. With her head thrown back against the wall, eyes squeezed tightly shut, she could have been in pain, but those tight spasms around his cock weren't spasms of pain. He couldn't hold back anymore, thank God, and came deep inside her, pleasure whiting out all other thought and feeling. She gasped again at the sensation of him climaxing inside her, and then sagged against him, her leg slipping down off his hip.

For a moment, they just caught their breaths. The noises of the party were suddenly very close. Had they just done this? Had he just fucked his wife in the supply closet at the annual office party? Sam grinned at the thought of it, the decadence, the insanity of this action.

Abby started to laugh, quietly, pressing her hand over her mouth. "Oh my God," she whispered. "Did we just do that?"

"Yeah. Yeah, we did." Sam carefully withdrew, his cock sliding from her warmth. "You're gonna be…kind of a mess."

Abby held her dress up, looking down at her legs now pressed tightly together. "Fuck, it's kind of hot, right?"

"What?"

She raised an eyebrow and gave him a tentative smile, nervous but laced with wickedness, letting the hem of the long black dress drop down to the floor. "Me, going back out to this party and talking to all these hot guys with your come still wet on my thighs?"

Sam's soft cock gave a hard twitch at that, mirroring the stab of arousal her words evoked. "Christ, Abby."

"You said you liked this side of me. So." Abby picked her panties up off the floor and carefully folded them into a tiny square. They were mostly lace, anyway. She tucked them into his shirt pocket, where they barely made a bump. "Can you smell me?"

So he had to crush her against the wall again, kissing her hard, one hand tangling up in those thick red curls. "You're killing me. If I could, I would fuck you all over again."

She returned his kiss, then gently pushed him away with her palms on his chest. "You really want this? You're really okay with me being attracted to other guys?"

"I really am." He tried to brush her mussed curls back into place. "Now, we need to get back before someone figures out where we've gone."

He shut the light off and opened the door a crack to peek out. The hall was clear, everyone in the main lobby and not, thank goodness, lingering around this hallway. Probably someone would be here if they'd been overheard. He cracked open the door and ushered Abby out, then followed a moment later.

"I'm going to head to the bathroom and freshen up," she said, smoothing her dress down. "Get me a drink, will you?"

No one was watching as Sam headed back into the main room. As soon as he'd reentered the main space, a somewhat familiar voice came from behind him. "Well, hi there."

Jo, Stephan's wife, was leaning against the wall right around the corner from where they'd been hiding, sipping some kind of cocktail. She was in the main room, but damn, she had been close by. Had she heard anything? Jo was unreadable, a perpetually playful expression on her face, and now she was as damn unreadable as ever.

"Nice to see you back. Stephan was wondering where

you'd run off to." She took another sip from her glass, looking overly casual. "I told him you'd be back in a few minutes."

He must have looked stricken. His face went cold, then hot, the color probably draining from it and then rising in a terrible blush. Abby was still gone, down the hallway near the bathroom.

"Oh, relax." She chuckled. "You think Stephan and I never snuck around somewhere we weren't supposed to? You have to do things like that. Keeps the marriage young."

"Right. I, uh…" Was he supposed to admit it? Deny it? He didn't know Jo that well, only through her husband. And, oh, damn, he and Abby had started off talking explicitly about *Stephan*. How much had she heard?

She didn't seem bothered. In fact, she seemed relaxed, casual, confident. Was this a woman who was about to ruin his life? What could she do, blackmail him? Was this something people blackmailed someone over? Threaten to tell Stephan that Sam wanted him to fuck his wife?

He was getting ahead of himself, and Jo's expression softened. "Look at you. Relax, relax." She looked around to make sure no one was listening. "You're way too worked up for somebody who just got fucked in a closet at a party."

Damn, he needed a drink. "This isn't something I normally do. Abby and I have just been trying a few things. Trying to spice up our marriage."

"Right." Jo nodded. She seemed to be measuring him up. "I don't know you that well, Sam. But Stephan says you're one of the best people he's ever worked with. I know he appreciates your friendship."

That was a weird turn of the conversation. "Uh, thanks. Likewise, about him. I like him a lot."

"Yeah. Listen." She stepped in and opened her mouth to speak, then closed it again, like she thought better of it. "We're always looking for more friends outside of work. Especially friends who aren't as uptight as some of the old-school people in Mapleton." She smiled, and that smile could mean a lot of things. "Maybe we should all get together sometime? Go out to dinner?"

This conversation had gone in a strange direction. "Sure. Yeah. That would be good. I'd like that." Abby was coming back down the hallway, looking as prim and proper as ever, and no one would know that her panties lay tucked away in his breast pocket.

Jo looked back to see Abby approaching, and gave a little wave before turning back to Sam. "Great. I'll drop you a message." She patted his arm, and then stepped away, headed over toward where Stephan was deep in conversation with someone else.

Abby wore a puzzled expression as she returned. "What did Jo want?"

"Oh, she just… She said they'd love to get together with us sometime. Because Stephan and I are such good work friends and all."

Abby's brow furrowed. "Sam Burke, what did you do?"

"Nothing!" Should he even tell her about Jo overhearing them? Abby was into that, but she might be too embarrassed, and there was something strange about Jo's invitation. He didn't want to read too much into it, but overhearing someone have sex and then inviting them out to dinner was…well, he could draw some conclusions if he wanted to. Being wrong would be disastrous, though. "We were just talking," he added. "She'd been looking for us. She ran into me."

"Okay." Abby didn't look that convinced.

"Come on." Sam held out his arm for her and smiled, trying to make it look natural. "Let's go schmooze a little more, yeah? The night is young."

Chapter Eight

The social media message popping up on Sam's feed the next evening should not, actually, have been a surprise. He should have expected it from the conversation with Jo at the party. Still, seeing her name show up as a message request sent him reeling back to the night before.

Hey. She sent him a smiley face emoji. *You have a good time at the party last night?*

That might be a double entendre, or not, but whatever. *Yeah. It was a lot of fun.*

Even beyond the closet fucking?

Sam stared at the screen. Jo was probably on the other end of the phone laughing. Or...was she flirting? She was married, and she knew he was married, but he didn't know her that well, and maybe there was something else going on here.

I'm just teasing you, she added, not giving him a chance to reply beyond staring at the screen of his phone in disbelief. *But I wanted to talk a little more about what I said last night.*

Oh good. She was going to explain that she might have

been misunderstood, and wasn't actually propositioning them, and that maybe she was drunk, and there would probably be an apology in there somewhere.

Okay, he typed, not wanting to go too far and presume anything.

I overheard you and Abby in the closet.

That wasn't news. She'd already teased him about it last night and then again today. *I figured that out.*

The little dots on the screen indicated that she was typing, and typing for a while, too. Some sort of big message was coming through.

No, I mean I overheard all of you and Abby in the closet. I heard what you said about Stephan.

Ah, fuck. Fuck, fuck, fuck. He didn't normally swear much, but this was the time, and a whole litany of curses began running through his head. He started frantically typing, dragging his fingers all over the tiny screen of his phone. Why were these keys so small? *I'm sorry,* he began. *We got carried away in the moment…*

Before he could finish his message another of hers typed up on the screen. *I'm not mad. I think it's hot.*

Sam stared down at the screen again. He looked around the empty room; Abby was at the pottery studio tonight, but her presence lingered all around him, like she was watching the screen along with him. This sick sense of guilt and confusion welled up inside him. He deleted what he'd written so far. *What do you mean? I was typing up a huge apology.*

LOL, she replied, with another smiley face. What the fuck?

Stephan and I have an open relationship. We each can sleep with whomever we want as long as we communicate about it. I have a girlfriend, and he's gone on some dates with other women as well.

Sam tossed the phone onto the couch. Was everyone in

this whole town living a double life that no one could see? What was it with small New England towns? First Mitchell dropped that bomb on him that he was in a whatever-it-was-called relationship with two other people at the same time, and now his coworker and friend, the guy he'd been work buddies with for over a year, turns out to be in an open relationship. Everybody in this whole fucking town must be punking him.

I'm not sure what to say, he typed, picking up the phone again, because he might as well be honest. *I'm starting to think everybody in this town is into kinky sex things and I'm just figuring it out now.*

LOL. Jo's text came back right away. *It's a liberal college town. I'm a sex educator. You'd be surprised how many people have secret lives.*

He hadn't considered that. This part of the state, liberal and open-minded, was bound to be more open-minded in everything. *I'm still really embarrassed that you overheard us. It was inappropriate.*

Yeah, but inappropriate is kind of my thing. Wink face emoji.

He didn't want to give her the wrong impression, though. *We're not in an open relationship,* he typed, and then hit send and quickly sent a follow-up message. *Not really, not like that. Not like you and Stephan are.*

More typing on her part. *You seemed to be pretty into the idea of it. I want to know what you're interested in.*

He let his hands drop and stared at the television, some show about gold mining on in the background just for noise. What was he into? He'd been trying so many things lately, so many different experiments. He hadn't wanted Abby to feel bored by him. He hadn't wanted her to think she'd made a mistake settling for him. Now that they'd moved beyond that, though, and were actually expanding their whole sexual repertoire, he had to face this question. What, really, was he into?

I like to be dominant sometimes. We played a little with power exchange. He sent that message, stared at it on the screen, then added another one. *I like watching Abby enjoy herself, with me or with somebody else.* He sent that message and then elaborated. *I got to watch her with another guy recently and it was incredible.* That was an understatement, but it was enough to get started.

So is it about watching for you? She asked.

Was it? He certainly loved watching her, but there was another part to it, another deeper element of the fantasy that he hadn't brought up to the surface yet. Jo was just a person on the other end of the chat, and he could confess this in writing. *I like thinking about it, too. I like imagining someone else taking her the way I do.*

Was he oversharing? Jo was asking these questions, but he was just answering them without thinking too much about it. Maybe he should rationalize some of this away. *I don't know,* he added.

It sounds like you do know. And it sounds hot as hell. She sent a smiley face.

What about you? She should share, too. Her situation was different than his. *Why do you share Stephan?*

She typed for a long while, long enough that Sam got up to get a beer out of the fridge while watching the screen. Finally, a block of text came up all at once.

We have an open relationship because we don't feel we can meet all of each other's needs and shouldn't have to. I do sex education workshops and learned about polyamory, and it made sense to me. I talked it over with Stephan. He had some reservations at first about being with anyone else, but we worked through it. Our relationship has been open for five years now. I think it's made our partnership better.

Mitchell seemed to indicate the same thing when Sam talked to him. Maybe there was something to this idea of not limiting a relationship to two people. If he and Abby both wanted to have her sleep with someone else, shouldn't that be okay? Maybe it was more normal than he'd thought.

Is it hot for you? He typed. *When he's with other people?*

Not really, LOL, she responded. *But I don't mind one way or the other.*

What was in this for her, then, bringing this up in the first place? But then she typed again.

But I'm like you. I like to watch. If it's happening with me there, I really, really enjoy it.

Sam's dick twitched, beginning to harden. What if they were both watching? He and Jo, watching Stephan and Abby together? The stuff of fantasies, right there. He couldn't get too far ahead of himself, though. They hadn't actually broached the specifics. Jo seemed near it, talking around it, like she was going to offer this as a possibility.

Another idea occurred to him, though, suddenly and all at once. *Did you tell Stephan?* If she had, if she'd brought this up with him, how would Sam ever face the guy again?

No. I wanted to talk to you first. Find out if this was a fantasy or something more. She then added, *So which is it?*

He could play this off as a fantasy and end this conversation now. From the way his heart was racing, that was probably the smartest idea. But instead, he was already typing. *It's not just a fantasy.*

She responded fast. *Good. I think we should set them up to be alone together.*

Well, that was…immediate. While he paused, she kept typing, the fragments coming one at a time but immediate.

If she really wants to be with Stephan
and you like the idea
and Stephan likes the idea

Then she should go through with it.

It read like a poem on the page.

I don't know if she'd go along with it, he typed. *And you don't even know if Stephan is interested.*

LOL, Jo replied. *I know Stephan. He would be interested.*

Was this all too fast? Sam wanted this for Abby, and he wanted this for himself. He wanted her to get everything she wanted, and he loved the thought of somebody else discovering how amazing she was. She was incredible in bed. Having her go out and sleep with someone else was a whole different level from what they'd done.

Abby was hot as hell, and knowing she was off sleeping with another guy was even hotter. Not just sleeping with another guy, but doing it because he told her it was all right, because he was getting off on the idea of her pleasured by someone else. Yeah, that was pretty damn sexy.

Okay, he typed. *So what do we need to do?*

• • •

Jo and Stephan were all smiles as they greeted Abby and Sam in the entrance of the Redfish Grill. "I'm so glad you could make it," Jo said, hugging each of them in turn. Sam had been pretty mum about the whole purpose for their going out to dinner, saying it was just to make some more couples friends together, and any of Abby's suspicions were immediately offset by guilt about those suspicions. They had very few "couples" friends. Sam really liked Stephan, and Jo always seemed nice on the few occasions Abby had to spend any time with her. Going out to dinner was a nice way to get to know people.

Of course, Abby also liked Stephan, and in a different way than Sam. The reminders of that fact rushed back into her body as he leaned in to hug her, holding her close against him for a moment. Sure, that was a normal greeting for friends, but damn, her whole body lit up like a Christmas tree from the inside.

"Thanks. It's nice to get together," she said into his chest. She could manage to be articulate today, even wrapped in his arms. With no alcohol in her system and time since last weekend to compose herself, she wasn't a horny wreck. Stephan was gorgeous, sure, but her lusts needed to be contained to unmarried, available people. Even if this one felt firm and warm against her, and smelled amazing.

Sam's body pressed against her as they slid into a booth. Stephan sat across from her, and Jo across from Sam. As they decided on food and drinks, conversation stayed light, mostly discussing the weather and what was happening at work for each of them. Eventually, though, after they'd ordered and passed through the less meaningful topics, Stephan rested his chin on one hand and looked across the table at Abby.

"So, Abby." Stephan fixed her with those dark eyes. "What do you do besides work? What are your passions?"

This was a normal way to ask people about what they were into, albeit with some provocative language, so she shouldn't read anything into it. "Pottery," she said, playing with the napkin on her lap. "It's my main art outlet now. I do mugs, plates, vases, that sort of thing."

"Do you sell them?"

"No. I thought about making it a business, but then it wouldn't be an escape. It would just be more work." She shrugged.

"Abby started college as an art major, actually," Sam chimed in.

"It's such a hard industry, these days." Jo nodded sympathetically. "Jobs are hard to come by."

"Actually, it wasn't the job. I had an internship that offered me full-time work after graduation, but it was sucking the joy out of art for me." She brushed her hair behind her ear. "I switched to something technical. For me, I wanted art to stay a hobby."

"Sometimes you have to divide it up like that." Stephan stroked his chin. "Your job, your passion, they don't have to be the same thing. One career doesn't have to be everything to you."

"Like people," Jo added. "It's why Stephan and I have an open marriage."

Abby fumbled her water glass, ice clinking against the sides as liquid spilled out over her fingers. "What?"

"An open marriage." Jo looked to Stephan, then across the table at Abby and Sam, her expression calm and pleasant as if she'd just told them the weather. "One person not having to be all things to all people."

"I...don't know why you just told us that." Abby tried to laugh, but it sounded strangled.

"Well, we're getting to know one another. That seems like something you're going to figure out sooner or later." Jo looked over at Stephan. "Right?"

Stephan was laughing as well, but his sounded genuine. "You really put it right out there, Jo."

"Subtlety is usually a waste of time, in my opinion." Jo sipped her water. "What about you, Sam?"

"What?" His eyes widened, and he glanced between Abby and Jo. "What about me, what?"

"What are your passions?" Jo smiled cheekily. "I'm not asking if you have an open marriage."

"We don't," Abby said quickly, too quickly, her words hard on the heels of Jo's. The attention shifted to her, and her face burned with a sudden blush. "We...are just with each other."

Sam's gaze bore into the side of her face, and she finally looked over at him. He was staring at her with his eyebrows raised. He was waiting for her to correct herself, or give more info. She looked down at the plain tablecloth. Couldn't the food show up and save her from this?

"Well, we're only with each other romantically," she added. "The rest is probably not the stuff for just getting to know each other." She laughed again. She had to stop doing that; it sounded terrible.

"I like a lot of things," Sam said, answering the question that had actually been asked. "I'm really into CrossFit. I play video games. I dabble in the guitar, but I'm not really good at it."

"You're good at it." Abby hated when he was down on himself. "Better than me, anyway. But I guess that's not saying much. Music is not my thing. I'm a visual arts kinda girl. What about you, Jo?"

"Climbing," Jo said.

Sam furrowed his brow. "Stairs?"

"Rocks, probably," Abby laughed. "Right?"

"Yeah. There's a rock gym here in town I go to this time of year, and when the weather's nicer, I climb outside. It's how I met my girlfriend, actually." She beamed.

Jo had a girlfriend. Stephan didn't even seem bothered by this. Abby was having trouble wrapping her mind around it.

"I've never tried that. Climbing, I mean." Abby could kind of picture herself giving it a go, though. "It seems kind of cool. I used to climb trees when I was younger. And smaller."

"I could take you some time. I'm always looking for new people to climb with."

"Sure, maybe."

Next to her, Sam shook his head. "And you still won't come to CrossFit with me."

"Do not start with me." She looked sideways at her husband, giving him her best stink eye.

He laughed, reaching an arm around to squeeze her against him. "Nah. I'm teasing. If you want to climb the walls, you go for it."

"You could come with us, you know." Jo winked at him across the table. "The more, the merrier."

Sam glanced at Stephan, who held up both hands in front of him in a defensive gesture. "Fuck no, don't look at me. Jo stopped asking me years ago. I'm terrified of heights."

"He is. You know, we went to the Grand Canyon last year, and he wouldn't go anywhere near the edge." Jo's smile teased affectionately, and she gave him a little shove with her elbow.

Stephan shook his head emphatically. "You're damn right I wouldn't go near the edge. That canyon is old as hell, and I want to live to be just as old. I was perfectly happy to see it from a few yards away. Still just as impressive."

"If you say so." Jo smiled with her tongue poking out the corner of her mouth. "One of my dreams is to go climbing out west. I keep telling Stephan he can come with me."

"I could go west. I'll look at rocks. But I will keep my feet firmly on the ground." Stephan lifted his chin toward Abby. "Take Abby. Drag her up a cliff. Sam and I can go do something else."

"I've never been out west." Sam looked over at the two of them, his eyebrows drawing together as he frowned thoughtfully.

"My family's originally from New Mexico. We're Southern Paiute. Stephan and I go back and visit them every so often." Jo looked past Abby's shoulder. "Finally. Food's here."

In the first few minutes of quiet after the food arrived, when they were all starting to eat, Abby mulled back over what Jo had said. What would it be like to go on vacation with another couple? They always went places alone, just the two of them, but people traveled with friends all the time for fun. It wouldn't be weird or even have to be sexual.

Even if she couldn't help having some new dirty thoughts when she looked across the table at Stephan. Sam had to know what she was thinking, but he didn't say anything.

"So what about you, Stephan?" Abby was careful to sound nonchalant. "What are you into?"

He grinned, and it was a naughty grin. The grin enough was enough to send heat into her face, but she wouldn't let herself look away. There was no reason to look away. Finally his expression softened into something less overtly flirtatious, and what the hell had *that* been about?

"I'm an artist, too. Like you. I blow glass."

"That's amazing." Her nervousness fell away. "I've always wanted to see somebody do that."

"You should go see his studio sometime." Jo took a bite of her chicken, gesturing in midair with her fork again as she chewed and then swallowed. "It's really cool. He could show you some things."

"Oh. Yeah, maybe." The thought of being alone with Stephan at his studio sent all sorts of feelings running through Abby's body, settling in her stomach. That wasn't what all of this was about. This was about Sam as much as her. Going to Stephan's studio, alone, that was probably innocent, and she was being a pervert thinking it was anything else. The fluttery feeling was replaced by guilt.

"You should." Sam looked over at her, his expression serious, and she felt even guiltier. "You'd love that. Glassblowing is amazing. Go, let Stephan show you a few things."

"I don't think we need another expensive hobby." She tucked her hair behind her ear again, a nervous habit Sam could probably see right through. "But I'd love to see it sometime, sure."

"How about later this week?" Jo looked over at Stephan again. "Don't you have the studio to yourself on Thursday?"

"Yeah. Thursdays are good. Abby, you could come over this Thursday if you wanted."

"Oh. Thanks. Yeah, maybe." This felt…weird. Sam was acting totally normal, but didn't he realize he was offering to send her alone to a studio with a guy she found hot? What the hell was he playing at? "Anyway. Have you guys watched any good shows lately?" Her voice sounded higher than normal in her ears.

"Abby, are you all right?" Jo paused in cutting her meal.

"Just warm all of a sudden." Abby fanned herself.

"It *is* warm in here." Sam reached over and set his hand on her leg. His touch started gentle and reassuring, and then he moved his hand to her inner thigh, and upward, sliding up beneath her skirt and lingering perilously close to her pussy. She smothered a gasp by pressing her lips together. Nobody else seemed to notice.

She was so focused on Sam's hand on her thigh that she hadn't even realized the conversation had changed.

"Can I ask you a few things about your open relationship?" Sam asked. "Since you brought it up, I mean."

"Sure." Stephan carefully sliced through his steak. "We're an open book. Or Jo is, anyway."

"Abby and I have been trying a few things and figuring out what interests us. Is there anything that surprised you about opening up like that? Anything you weren't expecting?" He finally moved his hand back to his own lap, leaving her to catch her breath and try to eat something.

"Probably the guilt." Stephan ate a bite of steak before continuing. "I thought I'd be jealous, but I was less jealous than I thought. Instead, I was worried Jo would be jealous, and feeling guilty."

"I'm not the jealous type." Jo shrugged. "I never really

have been."

"I can understand the guilt." Abby played with the napkin in her lap. "I sometimes feel like…" She let her voice trail off. The others waited, no one pressuring her to continue, eating while she gathered her thoughts. "I feel so worried about doing something wrong. I don't want Sam to think he's okay with something and then change his mind and I hurt him."

Sam squeezed her hand this time, closing his fingers over hers. "You're not going to hurt me. I love you."

Abby rolled her eyes, exaggerated. "Ugh. Gross."

They all laughed, the tension fading. Sam squeezed her hand again and held on for a long moment, reassuring her with his touch. "So where else do you folks like to go on vacation?" he asked.

Abby let out a breath. This was a much better topic. She could sit here and talk about normal things, and all would be right with the world.

Eventually.

Chapter Nine

"Thanks for meeting me." Sam stretched his tense muscles, shaking out his legs, breath puffing in the gray light of early morning.

Mitchell nodded, kneeling down to tie his car key onto the laces of one sneaker. "Nobody ever wants to come running with me at this hour. It's nice to have some company."

"Well, it's cold as fuck out here, so that makes sense."

They settled into an easy jog, figuring out each other's pace. Sam generally preferred CrossFit to running, but he still tried to switch things up now and then, and his body settled easily into the familiar rhythms. Somebody kept the rail trail treated all winter, and salt crunched beneath their feet as they jogged along. The morning was otherwise crisp and quiet.

Mitchell broke the silence, glancing over to Sam and then back at the trail in front of them. "I assume this is about you and Abby."

"Things have escalated." That was putting it mildly. Last time he'd talked to Mitchell about this was before Zach.

He'd only been trying to wrestle with power exchange back then. He tried to put his thoughts into words, and Mitchell just waited, jogging alongside him without pushing him. "It started with that vibrator I bought. So, we went to this dance club." Slowly, the story trickled out, without the salacious bits, the overview about Zach and then Stephan, as much as he felt like he could share about Abby's uncertainties without betraying her secrets. "And now, she's going to Stephan's glassblowing studio tonight."

Silence next to him made Sam look over, surprised to see Mitchell grinning. "What?"

Mitchell chuckled. "You're right. Things have escalated. How do you feel about all of it?"

He'd been asking that question to himself over and over. "Good. It feels big. And fast. And a little overwhelming. But I feel good about it."

Mitchell nodded. "I know those feelings."

"Does it ever stop?"

"It gets more normal over time." Mitchell smiled. "It still doesn't feel real sometimes. We're building this life together, and there aren't roadmaps. Even other polyam people, everybody does it differently." He caught his breath for a few steps before continuing. "Open relationships, hotwifing, triads, quads, intimate networks, there's so much out there. All these paths, all just trying to find our own way."

"It's good to know people. To have friends I can talk to." Without them, Sam would probably just be Googling things on the internet to no end.

"Same." Mitchell nodded. "You and Abby should come over sometime. Meet the family." He smiled. "It's still weird to call them the family."

"Definitely." He'd met them all separately, now, but it would be great to see them all together.

"Tell Abby she can't fuck any of us, though. We're a

closed triad."

Sam whipped his head around toward Mitchell, stumbling before catching himself, while Mitchell guffawed. "I'm giving you shit," Mitchell said, clapping Sam on the back.

Sam smiled in return, regaining his footing. "I'm starting to think you're kind of an asshole sometimes."

Mitchell nodded. "That's how you know we're friends. You still coming out for drinks with us tomorrow after CrossFit?"

Strange that some things could still be normal, when everything else was turning upside down. "I wouldn't miss it."

· · ·

All studios kind of looked the same. Walking into Stephan's glassblowing studio, Abby immediately noticed all the similarities to her own pottery studio: the urban-industrial vibe with metal lockers and steel tables, the wooden crates filled with tools, the lighting that never seemed bright enough. The only real difference, aside from the equipment, was the smell. The pottery studio smelled like clay, the faint tinge of glaze, and the light electrical burn of too many pottery wheels; the glassblowing studio smelled like fire.

Stephan didn't notice her come in at first. Hard at work at his bench, turning a small piece she couldn't really see over a glowing flame, he wore tinted safety goggles and a look of pure concentration. The room was a mixture of temperatures: cold winter air poured through the open windows, but the air closer to the tables was warm, and Stephan wore short sleeves. Not far from where he was sitting, a glassblowing oven flamed in the darkness, casting an eerie red light into the room and blasting heat in a very small area.

Her movement made him look up, and he smiled. "Just

give me a second to finish this."

"Take your time." Abby took her own time looking at him. There was no harm in looking, after all, especially when the subject of her gaze was absolutely gorgeous. Sam had been encouraging her to set her guilt aside about these feelings, and maybe she could. Looking wasn't touching. It was harmless. Eventually, he stopped his work and set the piece he was crafting aside.

Stephan turned off the torch, allowing him to push his safety goggles up into his hair. A faint sooty smudge marred his cheek, and she had to put her hands in her pockets to resist the urge to reach up and smooth it away. "Have you ever been inside a glassblowing studio?" he asked.

"Nope." She glanced around, which was safer than getting caught looking into his beautiful eyes. "Reminds me a lot of the pottery studio. Just with more fire."

Stephan grinned, and she caught his gaze. That was a mistake: he looked at her like she was the only woman in the universe. Sam could do that, too, make the world dissolve around them. She steadied herself against a wave of dizziness. Damn, he was handsome.

He pulled off his gloves. "You can hang up your coat over here."

Abby hung her jacket on the coat hook, then her sweater as well, since it was really warm in the studio. She was left in a cotton T-shirt and jeans.

"Natural fibers, just like I said." He smiled approvingly.

There was no real reason to feel proud, since all she'd done was literally follow the instructions in his text from yesterday, but his approval settled on her like a balm.

"I can do what I'm told," she said. Once the words were out of her mouth, she gasped. "I can't believe I just said that." She covered her eyes as they both started laughing. At least it broke some of the tension.

"It's okay." Stephan beckoned her closer. "I knew what you meant. Come on."

His hand burned hot through the thin fabric of her shirt as he touched the small of her back. He was too close, too intimate, suffocating her with his presence. This could easily be a platonic touch; his hand was closer to the middle of her back than the curve of her ass, but that small point of contact provided a constant distraction as he guided her through the stations. She forced herself to focus as he explained the types of tools, the difference between glassblowing and lamp work, then showed her the piece he was working on, a small curlicue for what would become a larger showpiece.

The oven was last, blazing heat forward out of the glory hole—which would never not be a funny word—and washing over her like it wasn't the middle of winter outside.

"I'm blowing a piece next." Stephan showed her the equipment he had set out for the task. "You want to watch?"

"Of course."

He smiled, warm and inviting, and Abby tried to ignore the rush of arousal. Moving away from him helped. Leaning back against the counter helped as well, as the cold steel pressed against her arms. God, why was it so fucking *hot* in here? It was freezing next to the door, but the heat from the oven pressed against her like a physical force. Stephan's hair was damp, a few curls wet against his forehead, and it looked...really fucking sexy.

Shit.

Trying to set her ridiculous hormones aside, she focused on Stephan's work. It was easy to become mesmerized. She watched in wordless, rapt enthrallment as he shaped the glass, spinning it in the flames in the oven, removing it, adding additional embellishments, eventually blowing it into a shape through a steel pipe. Watching someone do something they were really good at was its own kind of erotic.

Eventually, Stephan broke the piece away from its support, hitting hard enough that it seemed like the glass must shatter, but instead it separated perfectly. He set the piece to cool, so close that she could, if she wanted, reach out and touch it.

Stephan smiled at her. "Don't touch it."

He meant the piece, but he might as well have been talking to her about himself. "I won't touch it. I'm not an idiot." She tucked her hands into her jeans pockets.

"Sometimes it's tempting. Looking like it does right now."

She side-eyed his physique, attractive in the casual, beat-up clothes he was currently wearing, probably irresistible in a suit. "Yeah."

Stephan sat down on a stool next to her. "You ever think about trying it?"

With her attention split as it was, she had to pause to catch his meaning. "Glassblowing?"

His grin widened. "Yeah, glassblowing."

"I don't know. I like pottery. This is gorgeous, but I'm not sure I could create anything like that."

"Nobody does, at first. I have a whole shelf of terrible first drafts of things, and those are just the ones I kept instead of smashing and melting down." His smile invited her in, welcoming her. "You know, Jo is really hoping you'll go climbing with her."

Suddenly shy under his gaze, Abby ran a hand through her hair. "It seems like it could be fun. You ever do it?"

Stephan chuckled. "Once. I got halfway up the wall and swore never again. I really am deathly afraid of heights."

"Aren't you wearing a harness, though?"

Stephan shook his head. "This fear is not logical. The body wants what it wants, and my body wants to be firmly on the ground."

Abby studied those dark eyes, the line of his nose, the fullness of his lips. So many fears weren't logical…and so many were. *The body wants what it wants.* She could so easily kiss him, right here, in this glassblowing studio, with no one else around to see.

"I'm gonna step outside." Abby gestured toward the door. "I think I heard my phone." She was already hopping off the stool and grabbing her coat. She had to distance herself, escape from the heat of his body in this tiny, intimate, sweltering space.

The cold air outside hit her superheated skin like a slap as she stepped outside. With shaking hands, she dialed Sam. The steel door of the studio separated her from Stephan, and around her, snow fell on the gravel walkway. She walked a few feet away, back into the parking lot, out from under the overhang of the building. As the phone rang in her ear, she looked out at the emptiness of the space, their cars the only ones in sight. This studio sat on the outskirts of Mapleton, off a side street, the sounds of traffic too distant to hear.

"Hey, hon. What's up?" Sam's voice grounded her, anchoring her in this moment, even though her head was swimming.

"Why did you and Jo tell me to come to this studio tonight?"

A long silence from his end of the phone. "What happened?"

So much happened, and nothing happened. "Nothing. Nothing happened. I took a break to come out here in the parking lot and call you."

Sam sounded guarded. "I don't know why you're calling."

"Why did you tell me to come see Stephan here alone?"

Another long silence, his soft breathing the only sign that he hadn't hung up. "Stephan's a good guy."

Suddenly dizzy, Abby walked over to her car and leaned

against it. After the heat of the studio, the temperature difference overwhelmed her senses. "Did you want something to happen? Did you think I was just going to cheat on you?"

"Of course not." He sounded impossibly calm, even a bit cautious. "I thought you might call."

What? He thought she was just going to call him and… "And what? And ask about fooling around with him?" Words started tumbling out. "I don't know how I'm supposed to feel. Or what I'm supposed to do. Are you setting me up with him? Does he think I'm coming here to get laid or something?"

"No!" Sam sounded surprised, almost offended. "I thought…"

"Is Jo in on this? Is Stephan?" She didn't say it like a question, but like a fact.

A long pause. "Jo overheard us at the party. She approached me afterward to see if we might want something more."

Abby buried her face in her hands, embarrassment bubbling hot inside her. "So Stephan knows?" Is this why he had been touching her, working her over with those bedroom eyes?

"Yes."

Her stomach dropped. "I can't believe you didn't tell me."

"I didn't think you'd go. I thought, maybe once you were there in person…" His voice trailed off.

"I'd what? I'd just get overwhelmed? I'd let my hormones take over? I'd turn into some kind of raging slut who doesn't believe in her marriage anymore?" Her voice had gotten louder, echoing into the empty space around her. She was on the verge of hysteria and tried to tamp down the emotions.

"Abby. Abby, listen." Sam's voice was firm and steady in her ear, and if she closed her eyes, she could picture him next to her. "I love you. I know you love me. I know that you would do anything for our relationship. Right?"

"Yes."

"And I also know that you're attracted to other men. That you've ignored your attraction for years, that you would ignore it forever for the sake of our marriage."

Her throat was too tight to respond, but he didn't wait for her confirmation to keep talking. "I don't want you to ignore it," he said. "I don't want you to ignore your feelings for Zach, or for Stephan, or anyone else that you're attracted to."

"It's just…" She waved her arm around, even though they were on the phone and he couldn't see her. "I feel guilty. I needed to come out here and call you before I did something I would regret."

Another pause. "What if you didn't have to regret it?"

How could she not regret it? "I don't want you to encourage this out of some sacrifice for me. I don't want you to send me off to…to…" She forced the word out. "To sleep with other men, while you're sitting at home wondering."

He paused. "What if I find it really hot to think about you with someone else?"

She sagged against the car. "You're not here to watch."

"I know. But you could tell me about it after. That actually…" He paused, then started to chuckle, and his next words came out like a question. "It actually really turns me on? Like, *really* turns me on. At least as much as being there."

"Fuck, Sam." Abby sank down to the gravel. "I don't want to push you. I don't want to ruin what we have."

"Do you want to go back to the way things were?" he asked.

Did she? Did she want to just leave, and pretend this whole escalating experiment had never happened? "I don't think we could."

"But if we could. Would you want to undo it all?"

They'd done so much since New Year's, when they'd first tumbled headfirst into their mutual kinks. The new direction was uncertain.

But at the same time, she'd never felt so alive.

"No," she said at last. "I wouldn't want to undo it."

"Me neither."

Abby let out a shaky breath. "You really want me to go through with this? With Stephan?"

"If you're okay with it, yes. I want that." He sounded so sure, so confident.

"And Jo is okay with it, too?"

"You know she is."

"But what about after? What will this mean for us, and for the future?"

"Whatever we want. It could mean nothing at all." She heard the sounds of shuffling, as though Sam were getting into a different position or adjusting his phone or something. Picturing him in her head, sitting there, talking to her, was almost like having him here. He cared about her. He loved her. And he wanted this. "You don't have to do anything, Abby. But you could. It's okay. It's more than okay. I trust you."

"Okay. I… I don't know. I'll think about it." She paused. "I love you."

"I know." He sounded like he was smiling as he spoke. "I love you, too."

With the phone back in her jacket pocket, she stayed seated in the gravel and tilted her head back to look up at the sky. Tiny pinpricks of cold landed on her skin like icy reminders of her body, her sense of self. She knew what she was going to do. She knew it from before she hung up the phone with Sam.

Stephan was working in front of the ovens when Abby went back inside. He still had the same focused look, turning a glass ornament in the oven, spinning it while staring into the light through his glasses. He was so beautiful. Being attracted to Stephan didn't mean she wasn't attracted to Sam as well. Maybe this was okay. Maybe none of this was as serious as she wanted to make it out to be. That thought remained in her mind as she took off her jacket and hung it up once more.

Stephan had to know she was standing there, but he was in the middle of a task, and he completed it as she walked closer to the table between them. He moved with precision, and when he finally detached the piece from the rod and set the equipment aside, he did so with the same laser focus he had showed through the entire process. Then, setting his glasses on the table, he locked eyes with Abby. They stood staring at each other across the width of the long steel work table.

"Did you talk to Sam?" He'd guessed who she had called and probably why.

She thrust her hands in her jeans pockets. "Did Jo tell you?"

Stephan smiled lopsidedly. He clearly knew what she meant. "I told Jo, actually. I told her I found you hot and asked her how she felt about it."

Abby swallowed. "When was this?"

"After dinner."

After Abby and Sam had confirmed they were trying out some sexual adventures. "And what did she say?"

"You already know that." Stephan began to walk toward one end of the long table that divided them. Abby watched him, her heart crowding her throat.

"How do you feel about me, Abby?"

He approached slowly, rounding the end of the table. Now that she was staring into his eyes again, she couldn't look away, and all the words had dried up in her throat.

"Are you attracted to me?" he asked.

Stephan walked right up to her and she backed up, bumping the edge of the work table. They were close enough to touch. She nodded.

"What did Sam say?"

Abby swallowed. "You already know what Sam said."

Stephan licked his lips. He reached up and traced a fingertip along her jawline, the light touch making her shiver. "And what do *you* say?"

This was the moment where she could say no, or stop, and he would walk away from her. Everything was different from Sam: his scent, his height, his touch, even the very energy between them, but those differences triggered an excitement building up inside her like a tangible itch beneath her skin. She tipped her head back and parted her lips, watching the way Stephan's mouth mirrored hers, and then she grabbed the back of his neck and pulled him down to kiss her.

The heat of his mouth on hers contrasted sharply with the cold of her skin, chilled from her time outside. Abby closed her eyes, reveling in this sensation. Touch. His lips were soft, gentle, not insistent and firm or persuasive. Instead, he led the kiss like a dance: his lips teased hers open, and then his tongue brushed her lower lip, delicate, playful, inspiring her to kiss back in the same way. His biceps flexed beneath her hands. Under her touch, he felt solid, not strong in the same way as Sam, but present and real and kissing her like a man who had all the time in the world.

When he stepped back, it took Abby a moment to open her eyes and return to this place, this time. Stephan was still so close, kissing distance, and now that she had taken that first step, she wanted more.

Stephan leaned in again, but instead of kissing her, he closed his teeth on her earlobe and gave her a gentle nip. Her body quaked from head to toe at the contact. "I want you to call Sam," he murmured.

"What?" Her voice came out as a whisper.

"I want you to call him and ask him if he wants to listen."

Fuck. Abby made a strangled noise, and she got wet just at the thought. She fumbled the phone, trying to press the right contact while Stephan's hands inched her T-shirt up over her hips and skimmed around to the front of her jeans, already fiddling with the button. It was so damn hard to breathe in here.

"Abby?" Sam's voice sounded concerned. He had, after all, just talked to her, and he could probably hear how heavily she was breathing.

"Hi. Oh," she gasped, because Stephan took that moment to reach beneath her shirt and cup her breasts, his touch electric. For a second, she couldn't remember why she called, and then it all came flooding back. "Do you...want to listen?"

He swore harshly, his voice suddenly raw. "God, yes." He sounded like he was shifting position. Maybe he was touching himself already, or at least freeing his cock from his pants, and that thought turned her on even more, especially in conjunction with the way Stephan casually began rolling her nipples between his fingers through her bra.

Stephan patted the table behind her. He was already tugging her jeans down her thighs along with her underwear, and she climbed up onto the edge of the table with her feet dangling. Stephan finished pulling off her bottom layers, taking her shoes with them, and suddenly she was naked from the waist down. He pushed her legs to the side and got down on his knees in front of her. Looking up, he gave her another devilish smile. "Tell him what I'm doing to you." Then he slowly leaned in and dragged his tongue up against her clit.

Abby moaned loudly, brokenly, a sizzle of touch sparking outward from that tiny point of contact.

"Tell him," Stephan repeated, and did it again.

"He's licking my clit." It came out like a sob, and she couldn't sit up anymore, had to lie back on one elbow on the table and clutch the phone to her ear with the hand that wasn't currently pressed palm-down like a lifeline.

In her ear, Sam cursed again, and she barely heard the telltale sounds of his hand moving over his cock, the slick sounds of flesh. Between her legs, Stephan continued to lick and suck her clit, taking his time, his teeth even brushing the tender bud every so often and making her hips buck up. It was nearly too arousing, too intense, her nerve endings firing rapidly.

"He's...sliding a finger in me. No. Two fingers." It was too much of a stretch for one. She was so wet, and the noises embarrassed and aroused her at the same time.

"You're so wet. I love how wet you are." Stephan's voice sounded distant, muffled from his position still between her legs. "And you taste so sweet. I've been dying to get my mouth on you. I could eat your pussy all night."

"Holy shit," she swore.

Sam was in her ear, just like he was there beside her. "Does it feel good? Do you like having another man go down on you?"

"Yes, my God." She let her head drop back, because keeping it upright was too much effort. Her orgasm was already building, starting down in her toes.

"Are you gonna come like this?" Sam sounded like he could come right now, too, his voice deep and rough.

"Yes, yes, he's gonna make me come." She sounded like she was crying, but this was taking all of her concentration just to talk, and the curl of Stephan's fingers up against her G-spot had her moaning brokenly once more.

"Let me hear you."

Abby lay flat on the table, dropping all the way onto her back, holding the phone loosely to her ear. Stephan was going to drive her all the way over the edge like this. He knew just how to fuck her with his fingers while sucking her off, and she didn't hold back the gasps and moans falling from her lips like wordless prayers.

Stephan whispered to her, his mouth still against her clit, but she heard him anyway. "Come on, beautiful. Come for us."

That was it. That mounting tension peaked, a spring coiled inside her body, holding her on the knife edge for an endless moment, and then everything unleashed at once. She cried out, riding that spiraling pleasure as she clenched and clenched and clenched around his fingers. He kept licking and sucking her through it, guiding her through the peak and the aftershocks, letting her down while she twitched and moaned into final silence.

Sam was crooning into her ear when she became alert enough to realize it. "You're so good. God, that was so hot. You made me come so hard. I came all over my hand. Was it good, sweetheart?"

"So good." She twitched as Stephan slid his fingers out of her, getting to his feet a bit stiffly but looking like someone who had just accomplished something amazing.

Sam's next words took her by surprise, coming low and husky in her ear. "Do you want to suck him off?"

She did. That seemed even more illicit than having him go down on her. "Yeah."

"Good. You hang up and go thank him properly. All right?"

She could tell from his tone that this wasn't an order. This wasn't a dip into power exchange. This was about her, and what she wanted, and Sam pushing her forward when she might not make the next move herself.

"All right." She paused, wanting to tell him she loved him again, but was this the time?

Into the silence, he said. "Yeah, I know. I love you too." She could hear the smile in his voice. "Go on."

Smiling back, Abby hung up the phone. Stephan was

standing at the foot of the table, looking smug and satisfied even though she was the only one who'd been pleasured. She slid down, finding her pants and underwear in a heap on the floor and pulling them up her hips, then dragging Stephan down for a kiss. It was easier, now, a simple action, just one next step. He went willingly and kissed her with the same contented laziness, even though when she rocked her hips against his, he gasped in surprise.

He gasped in even more surprise when she slid down to her knees in front of him. "Jesus, you don't have to…"

"I want to," she interrupted him. "Let me." She unzipped his pants and freed his cock, which was hard as steel, soft-skinned in her hands. Then she swallowed him down. He gripped the table behind her, leaning over to steady himself, but didn't grab her head. He was so sensitive, shifting his hips with each long suck she gave, throbbing against her tongue. The weight of him, so foreign from what she had been expecting, so different from her husband, was a tangible reminder of what she was doing. How funny that something like this, kneeling in front of someone and sucking them down, could make her feel so powerful.

Stephan was trembling. His legs quivered. She doubled down on her efforts, gripping the base of his shaft with one hand as she sucked at the top half of his cock, tasting the first slick salty drops of his arousal. "Fuck. Abby. I'm gonna … God, your mouth is incredible. Oh my God." He grabbed her hair, let it go immediately. "Sorry. I won't…"

She lifted her mouth off and looked up at him. "No. Do it." She smiled, then slid him into her mouth again.

Stephan gripped her hair once more, his fingers tightening reflexively as he approached his orgasm. She hummed her appreciation, which made him twitch again. Rather than pull back, she stayed where she was, and he began to thrust a bit into and out of her mouth, like he just couldn't hold back. Cradling his balls with her free hand, she marveled at how they tightened against his body, drawing close with his impending climax. Above her, he was making the most incredible, desperate noises, like he was losing himself in this moment as much as she had been, and God, she wanted to do this again.

He came with a cry, and she drank it down, swallowing fast, sucking him through his climax as he twitched and moaned, hand tightening painfully in her hair before he released it. There was nothing like taking a man all the way like that, and when she finally, carefully got to her feet, Stephan was still leaning heavily on the counter with his eyes closed, like he might not possibly be able to stand anymore. He took a moment before he drew himself together again, tucking his dick away and letting out a long sigh.

"Fucking hell, Abby. Did Sam tell you to do that?"

She blushed, another illogical blush given the circumstances. "He asked me if I wanted to, and I told him yes."

Stephan leaned against the counter. "You are something else." He pulled her in and hugged her, and the affection felt…perfect. Not too intimate, not too detached, but exactly what she wanted at this moment.

She pulled back and looked up at him. "So what now?"

"Well, do you want to try glassblowing?"

Abby laughed. There was no tension here anymore, nothing that made her worry about the future. "Not tonight."

"Then how about you and Sam come over for dinner sometime soon?" Stephan smiled. "It would be nice to talk someplace comfortable."

Talk. Right. She knew what this would be, and yet rather than being worried, she was only excited. "I'll check with him tonight."

• • •

Walking into her house that night, Abby's body hummed with the same level of anxiety as when she had walked back into the glassblowing studio that afternoon. She was still slick from Stephan's mouth on her pussy. She had sucked his cock, and she imagined she could still taste him. What would Sam say? What would he do? He had told her to go through with this. He had been into it on the phone. Now, though, he might have changed his mind. In the heat of the moment, people sometimes agreed to dumb things.

Sam was sitting on the couch, resting against the cushions, the television off and music playing throughout the house. His expression looked calm, relaxed, even serene, and he beckoned her over when she stopped in the doorway. Before she could say anything, or ask him about his feelings, he pulled her down on top of him and kissed her, open-mouthed and deep.

"I can taste him on you," he said against her mouth, and her pussy clenched once at the husky tone in his voice. "It's all I could think about. I need to get these clothes off you."

It happened so fast, him pulling at her clothes and her helping, because she wanted him, too, wanted him with the same intensity like if she had not just come hard an hour beforehand. He flipped her down onto her back and slid his fingers through her wetness.

"You're so wet. God, Abby, I want you so bad."

"Fuck me. Please." She needed him, his cock, the solidity of his body on hers to mark her. He scrambled out of his own clothes and climbed on top of her, hiking one of her legs up onto the back of the couch, her other leg trailing down onto the floor, and fucked into her in a wet, hard slide.

It was messy, brutal, deep, the kind of fucking that left marks, and Abby gripped Sam's back and tried to pull him into her even more. She was *his.* He was hers. They belonged to each other. She hadn't even realized she was saying anything until she heard him breathe out a choked laugh near her ear.

"Yeah. I'm yours. You can stop saying it."

Abby laughed, that desperate laugh of strung-out emotion. "You're mine."

"And you're mine." He kissed her, his cock buried all the way inside her, still rocking his hips to thrust steadily, breath after breath.

"Do you like when I fuck someone else?" She needed to hear him say it.

"Does it *seem* like I like it?" He punctuated his words with more rough thrusts, one per word, the kind of thrusts that shifted her back and forth on the couch.

She gripped his arms tight, fingernails biting into his biceps. "Say it."

"I want." He kissed her lips. "You." He kissed her again. "To fuck other people. And sometimes I want to watch and listen as some other guy fucks this tight pussy and explodes inside you."

Abby shivered, imagining the hot rush of that feeling.

"And then." He pulled back all the way, sliding entirely from her warmth. "I want to step up and fuck into you when you're loose and wet from him." Gripping her hips, he pushed hard all the way inside again.

She hadn't realized how close she had been, but that one hard thrust sent her spilling over the edge. Her orgasm rolled over her in a series of spasms, and the whole time, she imagined the feeling of Sam fucking her while she was dripping from another man. Overwhelmed, she rode out those waves as Sam thrust a few times more and then spilled inside her.

In the silence afterward, when they had cleaned up and

sprawled on the couch in the same lazy way, she rested her head back against the cushions and closed her eyes. "Do you really want all that?"

"Yeah." He was open and honest, now, direct eye contact and no guile to be seen. "I really want that. What about you?"

Abby nodded, then smiled. "You know, Angela said I was worrying about all this too much. She said I wasn't giving you enough credit, and I should see where things led. She's gonna be insufferable now. One 'I told you so' after another."

Sam laughed. "You know you don't mind."

Abby pursed her lips. "Then I guess there's no harm in continuing on this path."

Sam raised an eyebrow. "What did you have in mind?"

"Stephan invited us over for dinner. I think we should go."

Sam curled a lock of her hair over his finger. "I like the sound of that."

Chapter Ten

Stephan and Jo's house was a quiet, simple ranch on the other side of Mapleton, about ten minutes past the city, and as soon as Sam pulled into the driveway, his mixture of emotions ratcheted up to eleven. Abby had been pretty quiet next to him on the drive over, falling into the contemplative silence she sometimes gravitated toward when she was nervous. She wore one of her fuzzy sweaters and her dark jeans, her standard winter outfit, and she looked soft and touchable. Here, sitting in the driveway, he reached out and put a hand on her thigh. She turned to look at him, and oh. She wasn't nervous at all. She was practically vibrating, her eyes aglow and her expression eager.

He wanted to say something, some kind of weird platitude about still loving her or none of this mattering, but the fact was that it all *did* matter, and if she didn't know he loved her by now, the conversation they might have in someone else's driveway was irrelevant. So instead, he leaned over and dropped a kiss on her smiling lips, and then turned off the engine.

Jo opened the door smiling. "Come in. Come on in." She stepped aside, reaching out to hug each of them as they passed. He got a whiff of some light perfume that he leaned in closer to inhale.

"Stephan's just finishing dinner. Thanks so much for coming." She smiled warmly. "Let me show you around." She took Abby's hand and tugged her toward the other room, letting it go as soon as they were both following. Casual touch, casual intimacy. She was obviously a touch-centered person.

"It's not a big house, but we like it." Jo gestured around the living room, which was intimate, with a big cozy couch, an armchair, and one of those super-sized luxury beanbag sacks facing a television mounted on the wall over a fireplace. Drawn to the photograph collection on one wall, Sam wandered over there. Photos of Stephan and Jo dominated the collection, but there were other photos as well; a bunch were photos of Jo and a blonde woman. They were posing on the beach, or next to each other at the summit of a mountain, or dressed in climbing gear.

"That's me and Becca." Jo had walked up beside him and waved a hand toward the collection.

"So she's part of the family, huh?"

Jo shrugged a shoulder. "Sometimes." She smiled. "Becca's a lesbian. She and Stephan are friends, but not more than that."

"But she's on your photo wall."

"Well, yeah." Jo smiled. "She's a big part of my life."

He followed as she took them down the hall, pointing out the rest of the rooms, finishing in the spare bedroom.

Jo put her hands in her pockets. "We also use it as an office, but it's good when Becca stays over, or we get guests." As they followed Jo back down the hallway to the living room, Stephan called them in for dinner.

"Perfect timing." Jo walked into the large kitchen and

kissed Stephan on the lips. Stephan wore a raglan with the sleeves rolled up above his elbows, and he was also wearing a yellow apron with polka dots.

Sam smiled. "Nice apron."

Stephan looked down at himself and then grinned. "What? Polka dots are gender neutral, dude."

Over chicken cordon bleu roulades, steamed green beans, and roasted potatoes, Sam started to think this was too good to be true. "Do you eat like this every night?"

Stephan and Jo started laughing together. "Hell no." Jo looked over at Stephan. "He likes to cook fancy, but we never do it unless we have an excuse. If other people are coming over, he's got an excuse."

"Damn straight. Don't want to waste all this talent on just us."

Jo wrinkled her nose. "Fuck you."

Stephan chuckled. "You know I'll always cook fancy for you."

"Bullshit you will! You cook fancy for our friends and you cook normal for me."

He gestured to her with his fork. "Well, my normal is still better than average, so I think you win."

Jo rolled her eyes in a parody of dramatic exasperation and looked over at Sam and Abby. "He's lucky that he's so talented, or I would throw him out on his ass. But he's pretty good with his mouth, so I keep him." She waggled her eyebrows at Abby and cast her a mischievous grin. "Right, Abby?"

Abby fumbled her fork, dropping it onto her plate with a loud clatter. She looked up at Jo with an appalled expression on her face before turning to Sam, who could not stop from grinning. God, she was adorable. At his expression, she started to laugh, too, putting a hand on her forehead and staring down at her plate. "You guys are all a bunch of assholes. I can't believe you just brought that up while we're eating dinner."

"You've got to excuse my wife." Stephan, sitting across from Abby, reached out and touched her free hand where it was sitting next to her plate. She looked up at him and then turned her hand to let him hold hers. A small gesture of intimacy, and rather than sparking Sam's anxiety, it settled him. Watching Abby and Stephan felt sweet, and he hadn't expected that. "Jo has absolutely no sense of propriety," Stephan said.

"And that's why you love me." Jo grinned at Stephan and winked. Stephan was still holding hands with Abby, and Jo seemed completely undisturbed. Abby released his hand and picked up her fork again. Smiling, she returned to her dinner, and the conversation turned to the snowstorm that was predicted for later that week. Apparently sex was just something they were going to joke about now and then with no real repercussions. It was...strange, actually, how normal it felt.

They all helped clean up after dinner, putting dishes into the dishwasher and storing leftovers, despite Stephan and Jo's attempts to shoo them into the living room where they wouldn't have to help. Helping felt more natural. When they finally went into the living room, Stephan had already started a fire in the fireplace, cozy on this frosty night. They had a big soft throw rug and cushions in front of the fireplace, and Abby was drawn to it like a magnet, sitting down on a cushion with her back to the fire and sighing like a contented cat. Jo stretched out on the couch, leaning her back against Stephan, and Stephan sat beside her with one arm absentmindedly draped over her shoulder. Sam ended up settling down in the armchair, close enough to Abby where he could reach out and lightly brush his fingers through her loose red hair. She was lovely in the firelight.

Opening her eyes, she looked over at Sam with a sated indolence. "How can we get one of these in our house?"

"We save up a lot of money."

Sam stretched out his own legs toward the fire, crossing Abby's, until she pushed them away.

"Get your feet off me." Grinning, she shifted into a more comfortable position away from his feet. "Well, if we can't afford it yet, we'll just have to come over here and steal the fireplace from Stephan and Jo."

"You can't just *steal* our fireplace." Jo gave them a look of mischief, like the one she'd given them at the kitchen table. Clearly an instigator, that Jo. "You have to have something to barter with."

"Oh, is that so?" Abby leaned back, supporting herself on her arms, and tipped her head to the side. "So what do you folks accept?"

"Hmm." Jo looked at Stephan. "Hon, what *do* we accept in barter?"

Stephan waggled his eyebrows. "That's a pretty loaded question, don't you think?" The tension sizzled, like any minute now things were going to escalate, but they sat there at the precipice of where this evening was definitely going. This was a hell of a place to be, imagining what might come next and ready to roll with it. Sam had no real idea what, if anything, Jo and Stephan had planned, but this moment was about to happen, and he was ready for whatever it might be.

"You know..." Stephan looked over at Jo, who was watching with the kind of contented interest of a satisfied cat. She seemed smug, knowing where this was headed.

"I know what?" She tipped her head back to look up at him.

"I'm not the only one good with my mouth. Abby is pretty damn impressive." He smirked.

Rather than blushing like usual, Abby laughed, and Sam

felt a rush of pride that surprised him.

"Oh?" Jo leaned her head on her husband's shoulder and looked up at him. "I think I'd like to watch that." She turned to look at Abby, who was still gaping and blushing and, inexplicably, smiling broadly. "You know, Abby, Sam's right over there."

Abby looked up at Sam, and her eyes filled with longing, not embarrassment, but that consuming lust he loved to see on her. Slowly, she shifted up onto her knees and inched over to where he sat, licking her lips, and she was actually going to do this. Fuck, that took his cock from half hard to aching in no time, and by the time she got his zipper down, he sighed with the relief of having his erection freed from his clothes.

Abby's hot, wet mouth on his cock made him gasp and grip the armrests of the chair. He was getting a blow job in front of his friends, and they were watching like this was the most fascinating thing in the world. Stephan reached an arm over Jo's shoulder and ran his thumb across her nipple through her shirt, making her shift more into his touch and sigh. Sam looked away from them to look down at Abby, who was bobbing her head on his erection like she couldn't get enough of him. He didn't want to come yet, but it took all his self-control to hold off. Jo whispered something to Stephan before Stephan got up off the couch and knelt behind Abby on the floor. She lifted off Sam's cock in surprise, obviously feeling someone behind her. Stephan was there, waiting, and he cupped her face and brought her mouth to his. Watching another man kiss his wife was...unbelievable. She made this soft whimpering noise into Stephan's mouth, and Stephan started to pull at her clothing. Abby let him tug her sweater off, then the undershirt she wore, and he unfastened her bra with ease. She looked first up at Sam, then over at Jo, and then closed her eyes entirely as Stephan cupped both her breasts and began to caress them.

"Abby, your breasts are gorgeous." Stephan kissed her down her neck, and she shifted so she was leaning back against Sam's legs, her head lolling against his knee. Stephan worked quickly on the rest of her clothes while she breathed raggedly, dazed, reaching down to help when he couldn't get her jeans off. Before Sam could fully process what was happening, Abby was naked on the soft carpet in front of the fireplace, and Stephan had leaned down and taken one of her nipples into his mouth. She arched up, body tensing and relaxing with each stroke of sensation.

Jo had unzipped her jeans and slid one hand down the front of her pants, lazily touching herself with a relaxed expression on her face. She nodded her head toward what was happening on the floor, one eyebrow raised, and Sam licked his lips. Abby turned her head to the side, her expression dazed. She opened her eyes and gasped; Stephan had tucked a hand between her legs, and although Sam couldn't see exactly what Stephan was doing, he could definitely see the effect it was having on Abby. She was beautiful. Blissed-out, slowly dragged through her own arousal by someone else, she was the picture of perfection. Sam reached down to pinch the nipple that Stephan wasn't currently sucking and biting, making her squirm anew. She shifted her hips, arching into Stephan's hand, making pleasant, soft moaning noises.

"Stephan." Jo's voice sounded clear and calm from the couch, maybe a little breathless. She didn't stop touching herself as she talked to him, and everyone looked over at her, even Abby, who blinked a few times in a daze. "I want to watch you two fuck her."

Jesus Christ. Abby gasped and then moaned as Stephan rubbed her again. Stephan turned to Abby. "I want you on my cock. Do you want that?"

Abby nodded. "Yes. Please." She shivered. She looked up at Sam, turning her head, her eyes asking permission as if he hadn't already given her permission.

Stephan pulled his hand away, putting his fingers in his mouth immediately. The sight of that made Abby laugh breathlessly. "I can't think straight when I watch you do that."

Stephan grinned. "That's why I do it."

Sam stroked his hand through Abby's hair. "You should suck his cock."

Abby licked her lips, paused, and nodded.

Her sweet upturned ass presented a welcome sight as she turned to Stephan, who was sitting on the floor already unbuckling his belt. Swatting his hands away, Abby took over, freeing his dick. She wasted no time bending down and taking him into her mouth. Sam never really got to listen to the noises Abby made when she sucked cock; he was always too worked up by the sensation of her tight, wet mouth around him. Now, watching Stephan close his eyes and tip his head back, he was able to fully concentrate on Abby's small hiccuping moans and murmurs. Her pussy was right there, slick and aimed toward him, barely visible between her thighs. When he leaned over, he was able to easily slide two fingers into her warm wetness.

"Oh, fuck yes." Jo's voice from the couch made Sam turn. She was half undressed, her jeans pushed down around her thighs, one hand dipping in and out of her folds as she watched the sight on the floor in front of her. Sam turned his hand palm down, using his thumb to find Abby's clit and rub against it as he pressed his fingers into her pussy. She shivered and shoved herself back against his hand, fucking his hand as she sucked Stephan's cock. Another shifting noise from the couch, and Jo pulled her pants back around her hips and then stepped out of the room. Where was she going? She returned a moment later from down the hall, carrying something. She came and knelt down on the floor next to them, not close enough to touch, but it was still enough that Abby sat up abruptly, glassy-eyed and surprised. Sam took his hand away and let her sit back.

"It's okay." Jo held up the items, which were condoms and lube. Abby laughed, breathless.

"Yeah?"

"Of course." Jo smiled lopsidedly.

Abby turned to face Stephan, who was already grabbing a condom, and then back to Sam, her expression questioning. Behind them, Jo cleared her throat, and they all looked over to the couch.

"You know, I think I have something to make this much more interesting." From her fingers, she dangled a black blindfold.

. . .

With the blindfold on, Abby couldn't see as she was walked down the hallway, presumably to the bedroom. It was definitely Sam's hand in hers, his hand on the small of her back. Wearing the blindfold, she wasn't even self-conscious about being naked in front of everyone. With the sexual stimulation temporarily stopped, her mind was settling back into place, letting her wonder about and anticipate what was to come.

No one spoke. She trusted the people she was with. When her legs hit the soft edge of a bed, she carefully climbed on, feeling the blankets already pulled back and the sheets exposed. The bed dipped on either side of her, and she imagined Jo sitting in the chair in the corner and watching, just like Sam had done before. But then there were hands on her body, hands she couldn't see and could only feel, and she lay back and gripped the sheet below her and felt instead of thinking.

One mouth on her nipple, then another mouth on the

other nipple, hot, wet, sucking and biting, unevenly paced and keeping her on the knife-edge of confusion. She thought she'd be able to tell the difference between the two men, but she couldn't. It was just sensation, each moment coming too hard and fast for her to parse them out and separate them. Someone's hand was between her legs, rubbing her clit, more aggressively than she usually did but also perfect. She couldn't stop herself from making so many noises. Fuck, this had not been her exact fantasy, but *why not?* She should have spent way more time fantasizing about this.

She was being coaxed over onto her belly, so she rolled over, and then her hand was guided to a hard cock. Sam's? It felt like Sam's, but she couldn't be sure, and that made it even hotter when she leaned down and sucked it into her mouth. Surprising how difficult it was to tell them apart without looking, with the scents mingling, but not knowing was even better. Especially when a hand on the side of her head guided her off that cock and onto another. She was sucking each of them in turn, and she felt like such a slut in the way that made her absolutely soaked between her legs.

"Good girl," Sam crooned, and fuck, that could make her explode. She sat back and licked her lips, catching her breath and gathering herself.

Stephan's voice sounded just as strung-out as Abby felt. "I want to fuck your wife." He was talking to Sam, not to Abby, and that was a little crazy, that feeling of being used.

She laughed, feeling breathless and a little light-headed. "I want that."

Jo's voice reminded Abby she was there. "We all want that."

Abby toyed with the blindfold. "I think I'm done with this." She tugged it off. "I want to see what's happening." And, she had her own idea of what she wanted to happen. Normally, she'd been passive in this, and that had been part of the fantasy. But this was also her fantasy now, too. "Stephan, lie here." She patted the bed, and he stretched out on his back. She eyeballed the distance between him and the edge of the bed, and had him scoot closer. Perfect. Now, where were the condoms? "Condoms? Where's my purse?" She'd left everything in the other room.

Jo tossed her one, grinning. "There ya go." Jo was still clothed, sitting in the corner chair, obviously enjoying the show. Abby was done feeling self-conscious. She handed the condom to Stephan, and when he had rolled it into place, she straddled his hips, kneeling and facing his feet instead of his head, then slid all the way down to take him into her with one smooth stroke.

Stephan gripped her hips from behind, fingertips digging into the soft flesh there, his body suddenly tensing beneath her. "Jesus. I wasn't expecting that."

He did have a really great cock. The hard length filled her up, and she naturally wanted to move on it, rocking back and forth. She gestured for Sam to stand in front of her, at the edge of the bed, letting her lean forward to take his shaft into her mouth. He gasped, grabbing her hair for stability for a moment, and then began to gently thrust. Beneath her, Stephan shifted his hips, filling her up with his cock, and she had Sam's cock in her mouth, and she was stuffed from both ends. Holy shit. It was too much to concentrate on, too much sensation, compounded when Sam began pinching the nipples on her swinging breasts.

Stephan cursed. "Fuck. She squeezes me so hard when you do that."

"Good." Sam chuckled. He sounded breathless, too. Behind her, Stephan shifted, his cock suddenly pressing into her at a different angle. She lifted her mouth off Sam's dick to see what was happening. Stephan had stolen some pillows to prop up his torso, and in this position, he could reach around over her hips and stroke her clit.

"Ohh." She closed her eyes as a jolt of electricity ran through her body.

Stephan rubbed slowly, steadily. "Keep sucking him."

Abby leaned forward, carefully, because this was more precarious than it had been, the alignment of their bodies changed by the angle. Before she closed her mouth over his cock head, she looked up at Sam. "You can be rough with me."

His eyes went darker with lust. Smiling, she took his dick into her mouth again.

He carefully took her head between his hands, and she moaned her approval. Then, holding her steady, he began to thrust into her mouth.

Stephan began to thrust harder too, as much as he could in this position, and he rolled her clit in steady circles beneath his fingers. She could come like this, if only he'd go a little faster. He seemed to know, not increasing his pace, keeping soft and steady.

Stephan spoke to Sam. "When do you want me to make her come?"

"Damn." Sam sounded right on the edge. "Are you holding her there?"

"I can feel her squeezing me. I can feel her getting close. Do you want to come first? You want to make her ask for it?" Stephan was so fucking deliberate.

"You hear that, sweetie?" Sam stroked her cheek, and she moaned around his dick, because God, this was the sexiest fucking thing she'd ever felt. He pulled out, holding her under the chin. "That's what I want. I want you to make me come. I want to come in that sweet mouth of yours, and I want you to do a good job. Otherwise, maybe we'll just have to keep you all needy like this until we're ready to go again."

Abby shuddered all over her body, and that idea alone

was almost enough to get her off.

"That turn you on?"

She nodded, not really trusting her voice to speak. Sam stepped forward again and pressed his cock between her lips into the warm wetness of her mouth.

He might do it, too. He might keep her like this, teasing her. She'd seen that side of him, the side that got turned on having her needy and desperate. She sucked hard, using her hands to cup his balls. He was trying so hard to hold out, but she knew what she was doing, knew what drove him wild, and took him steadily to the brink. He came into her mouth and she swallowed it down, sucking him until he trembled and stepped back on wobbly knees. "Fuck."

Abby sat back, sinking back down onto Stephan's dick. He began rubbing her clit harder, and the pleasure started to spiral up inside her, building. She was mindlessly rocking against him now, driven by instinct, chasing that orgasm.

"Make her come," Sam directed, and the authority in his voice was all it took before she felt the climax crash over her body.

She could still feel what was happening, the sharp rush as Stephan kept rubbing her clit and kept her coming and coming, but words were gone and she was a single raw nerve ending throbbing with wave after wave of climax. She shuddered and clenched and clenched and clenched, and in the middle of it all, she opened her eyes and looked at Sam. He was watching her with the kind of lust that made her feel like the most desired woman in the world.

As soon as she was coming down, Stephan's hands dug into her hips, and he came inside her, only a condom between them. His body relaxed, and she carefully lifted off of him.

Abby sprawled out on the bed, catching her breath, and Sam came over and sat next to her. They both looked exhausted, she was sure. Stephan sat up, sighing, and got shakily to his feet to take care of the condom.

Jo got up from the chair, shedding layers as she went, stripping down to nothing. Stephan grinned at her, beckoning her over, Abby and Sam seemingly forgotten as she climbed onto the bed with them. God, it was a good thing they had a king-sized bed; they wouldn't all fit in a queen. Abby turned to watch. Jo, naked and unselfconscious, climbed on top of Stephan and kissed him full on the mouth, rutting against him. There was no way he was going to get hard again that fast unless he was some kind of superhuman. Instead, Jo climbed up his body and straddled his face, lowering herself onto his mouth with a sigh.

Abby's own arousal ratcheted up at the sight. Jo gripped the headboard and rode Stephan's face, grinding herself against his mouth, head tilted back and lips parted. It was live-action porn, literally two feet away from them, and Abby rolled over onto her side to face what was happening. Without speaking, Sam urged her to lift her leg up over his where he lay spooned behind her. He reached down through her curls and began fingering her. She had just come, but she wanted to come again, and she watched the scene breathlessly as Sam manipulated her clit and bit her earlobe. Faster than she expected, faster even than the woman in front of her, Abby tumbled into another orgasm as strong and fierce as the first.

She was just coming down when she saw Jo come. It was gorgeous to watch her in the throes of climax, fascinating and beautiful like it was in the best kind of porn, but realistic, not constrained by the limits of the screen and instead live and in front of her with its sounds and sights. She was captivated. Behind her, Sam kissed her neck, and she leaned into it, the drowsiness of her own post-orgasm feelings making her sleepy and slow.

Afterward, when it was all done, when they lay in couples on the sprawling expanse of the king-sized bed, Jo propped her head on her hand and looked over at Abby and Sam. "Everything you were hoping for?"

Abby hadn't even known what she was hoping for. "Definitely."

"Well." Jo sat up and stretched, arching her back before flopping back down onto Stephan's chest. "We can always do it again."

Abby surprised herself by laughing. Yeah, actually, they could. They could do this again. With them, and maybe with Zach, and anybody else they wanted.

Stephan rubbed his belly and yawned. "I'm starving."

Jo grinned. "We literally *just* ate."

"That was hours ago. And I did a lot of work. How about I make nachos?" He looked over at Sam and Abby. "You want nachos?"

Sam chuckled and sat up. "You make nachos, I'm eating nachos." He grabbed Abby's hand. She smiled and followed.

Chapter Eleven

Where the hell was she? Abby looked around and blinked, taking a minute to recognize the guest room in Stephan and Jo's house. The reminders of the night before came flooding back to her, memories of the intimacy and, holy shit, the sex, all of that feeling more like something another person would have experienced than something she really did. Her body was sore, but the good kind of sore, the "I just got fucked" kind of sore. She was smiling, too, and couldn't stop smiling.

Next to her, Sam stirred, sliding an arm around her and drawing her closer as he blinked awake. He smiled sleepily. "Hey."

"Hey." Damn, he was handsome. He had this lazy sleepiness about him, the groggy look of one just waking up but completely sated. Her heart felt like it might be too big for her chest. So much for her fears of the morning after. The morning after felt pretty good right now.

"I'm starving. You starving?" He propped himself up on his elbow and looked around, then fumbled for his phone on the nightstand. "Wow, it's almost eleven."

"What? Really?" Abby sat up. She never slept naked, but without having packed an overnight bag for this trip, it had seemed like the most natural option. She checked her own phone, which wasn't quite dead, even after having not been charged overnight. Sure enough, it was ten fifty in the morning. "Jesus. We never sleep this late."

"Well, we stayed up pretty late." Sam rubbed sleep from his eyes.

A knock at the door made them both turn. Abby's first instinct was to cover herself, but the ship had kind of sailed on that, hadn't it? "Come in. But we're naked."

Jo was laughing as she opened the door. "I appreciate the warning. We were thinking about grabbing brunch. You want to come with? You can also stay here and sleep if you want."

As if in answer, Sam's stomach gave a loud gurgle, and he looked down at it. "I think that answers that."

"Great. Oh, also." Jo disappeared from the door, then returned a moment later with a pile of clothes. "I washed your clothes."

"What? When? You didn't have to do that." Abby took the pile from Jo, still warm from the dryer.

"I got up early, thought you might not want clothes with sex all over them." She smiled broadly, then laughed. "You look stricken."

Yeah, Abby probably was making that horrified face, and she let it go and laughed as well. "Sorry. I'm just not usually so blunt about talking about this stuff."

"I think once you've seen somebody's bits, you've got to be a little more blunt." Jo flopped the clothes down onto the bed and then backed away. "You want to shower?"

Abby looked over at Sam, whose stomach gurgled again. "Nah. We're starved. Let's just go eat."

In the car, following Jo and Stephan as they headed to Sylvester's for brunch, Abby kept glancing over at Sam in the passenger seat. His hands folded in his lap, he wore a slight frown on his face that seemed more thoughtful than upset.

"What?" she asked after a little while of silence. "You okay?"

Sam made a little "Hmm" noise and then shrugged. "I don't know. I think so. I keep expecting to feel different, but I just don't."

"Yeah." Abby was having that same sense. It was jarring, the way normalcy seemed imbued in this morning that should have felt not-normal at all.

There wasn't time to talk further, though, because they were already parking. Sam took her hand as they walked up to the entrance, the cold biting into Abby's skin and reminding her that winter was not over by a long shot. For now, though, she felt warm inside.

• • •

They sidled into a booth in the corner, couples on each side facing each other, and Sam reached over to give Abby's thigh a squeeze. She had been hard to read this morning. Although she was all smiles, she had this odd look about her. Maybe she was going through the same questioning that he was.

"We come here all the time." Jo didn't even open her menu, keeping it flat on the table in front of her. "It's our favorite brunch spot."

"We love this place, too." Sam scanned the options, as he always did. "I try to vary it up a little, though. I never want to stick with the same meal every time we come."

"Well, variety is the spice of life, right?"

Jo's comment sounded cheeky, and when Sam peered over his menu, both she and Stephan were grinning like they'd collectively come up with the best and worst double entendre. Next to him, Abby chortled.

"You know, I don't know if I'm going to be able to get used to this direct conversation thing." She looked over at Sam.

"That wasn't very direct," Jo corrected. "It was actually just barely a hint."

Stephan snorted. "Yeah, if she wants to be direct, she'll just ask you if you had a good time fucking Sam and me last night."

"Jesus." Abby looked around. "Guys. We're at brunch. It's the least sexual meal of the day."

"Maybe the way *you* do brunch, it is." Jo raised an eyebrow. "But brunch for us is usually our favorite thing to do after partner swapping or going out on separate dates. It's like, hey, let's all check in. So." She folded her hands. "Let's check in."

The waiter came over just then, because of course he would. When he finally left, Abby let out a long breath, slowly exhaling while she presumably gathered her thoughts. "I had fun last night. I'm glad we did it." She glanced at Sam. "I wouldn't be opposed to doing it again. And…the rest, I think Sam and I have to debrief together."

"Of course." Stephan nodded. "For what it's worth, Abby, Sam, last night was awesome for me. I had a really amazing time. If you're ever down for that again, I'm here. Whether it's all of us, or just me and you two, or"—he looked at Abby—"just me and you, give me a call."

"Right. Thanks." She smiled, and it looked genuine. "Sam? What do you think?"

Multiple emotions ran through him in quick succession, but one persisted through all of them. "I think that last night is something to remember." He looked at all of them. "And to do again."

Jo smiled. "That sounds good to me." She folded her hands on the table. "Now, have you guys seen any good movies lately?"

• • •

Home felt weird. Well...not weird, exactly. Abby looked around as Sam followed her inside, shutting the door behind them. Home felt exactly the same, and she felt different. Not only well-fucked, but also psychologically different. And maybe it was silly to put such emphasis on sex, because it was just sex, but this seemed like a new step forward.

"Let's talk about this." She rounded on Sam even as he was just hanging up his coat by the door, and he gave her the wide-eyed expression of surprise.

"About last night? Now?" He swallowed visibly, then gave a nod-shrug. "Okay, yeah. So. I know you weren't necessarily thrilled about having another woman there."

"That was surprisingly not a big deal." She hadn't felt weird about Jo at all, except that it was unusual. "I don't want to fuck her."

"No." Sam smiled, and the warmth in his smile made her heart feel a little bigger. "And, to be clear, I don't want to fuck her, either."

"Okay." After wandering over to the couch, she sat down, drawing her leg underneath her. Sam sat beside her on the sofa. "I think in time, I might be okay with you dating someone other than me," she told him. "But I don't think I'm there just yet."

"I don't need you to be okay with that, ever." Sam reached out for her, taking one of her hands. His thumb grazed the back of her knuckles, soothing her. "I'm not looking for that. What Stephan and Jo have, it's hot, and it's great for them, but I'm not looking for it for me."

"And if someday you are?" It was possible, after all. These things changed and evolved.

"Then I'll talk to you. And we'll decide together what's right for us." He gave her a reassuring nod. "But that isn't what I really want to talk about."

"Oh?" What was there to talk about, if not sleeping with other people?

"We didn't really talk about what this might mean for us long-term." He stroked her thigh, once, and then took his hand back. "I like this. I like what we've been doing. I like what's happened to our sex life, and I really like watching you be this lusty woman you've been hiding all this time."

Abby rolled her eyes, but she also smiled.

"I want to know how you feel," he said.

That was the biggest question. She'd put this part of herself aside, and it felt weird to reconcile it with the way she was now. But she definitely didn't want to go back. "I want to keep going with this. With Stephan and Jo, and…probably Zach, and…I don't know. Other people. And I want the kink sometimes, and the playfulness, and maybe whatever weird-ass fantasies you've got kicking around in there."

Sam grinned. "You're okay with that? You don't think it's the kiss of death for our relationship anymore?"

"I guess I overreacted a little bit." She interlaced her fingers with his. Nothing was going to replace Sam, who was so deeply a part of her life that she would never want to separate them. But sex was different. Sex could be fun and not be the end of the world. They could be adventurous together, and with other people, and their relationship could maybe end up even better than before.

What was there not to like?

"I think," Abby said at last, "we should keep going just like we are. And see what happens."

Sam leaned her back onto the couch, kissing her like he had all the time in the world, smiling into her mouth. "I have another fantasy to tell you about."

"Oh?"

He dropped another kiss on her lips. "It's the one where we have wild, hot sex forever and our marriage just keeps getting better for it."

Abby rolled her eyes. "You're killing me."

"You love me for it."

She looked into those warm brown eyes. She'd underestimated their relationship. This was only the beginning.

"Come on, you weirdo." She nodded toward the bedroom. "I want to get you back into bed."

Epilogue

"Oh my God, I can't watch this." Sam exhaled a deep breath and turned away from the giant rock in front of him, facing out into the desert landscape instead. Beside him, Stephan shielded his eyes against the sun and shook his head slowly, gaze still focused on the woman climbing the sheer surface.

"It makes my knees wobbly from here." Stephan grinned, though, clearly not as shaken up as Sam. "Look at her go. She's really come a long way in just a few months, Sam. You should watch."

Sam turned back slowly. He had never had a real fear of heights, not the way Stephan did, but watching Abby climb this rock face inspired all kinds of tension inside him. He wanted to protect her from every possible danger, but she didn't need protecting. She needed adventure.

Damn, Abby really was impressive. She'd claimed this wasn't a difficult route, suited for beginners, but it looked pretty fucking challenging to him, who'd never climbed anything more difficult than a ladder. No matter how athletic he was, this was not exactly his cup of tea. Abby, though, was in her element, moving with deliberation. She reached carefully for another handhold, the red-orange rock covered in white chalk from previous climbers, and shifted her weight along with her feet. He'd watched her in the gym a few times, but this was different. Helmets, gear, a certain gravity—hah—to the way Abby and Jo interacted, all of it indicated that they'd taken a new step together.

Of course, all of this was a new step together, so many new steps these past few months, a friendship that kept deepening and developing the more time they spent together. He smiled to himself, because damn, a lot could change in a short period of time.

"What are you grinning at?" Stephan asked.

"I was just thinking." Sam thrust his hands in his pockets. "Six months ago, if you had told me I'd be here, I wouldn't have believed it."

"Which part?"

"None of it. The road trip, the rented RV, you and Jo, it's wild." Everything was crazy, and somehow the most normal part was watching his wife climb a rock face in the middle of the desert. Tomorrow, Jo's girlfriend Becca would fly out to join them, and the three women could scale more rock faces while he and Stephan talked shop and drank beer. Not a bad vacation.

Stephan smiled, that warm, crooked smile that told Sam everything was going to be okay. "Cross-country road trip with your fuck-buddy friends. It's a wild world, man."

A wild world indeed. And it wasn't just vacation, either. They had a whole new set of adventures waiting for them after they returned. Mitchell had encouraged Sam to compete in his first CrossFit tournament, which was coming up at the end of the month. Angela was taking Abby into New York for a girls' getaway weekend. What he was secretly looking forward to most of all, though, was Abby's upcoming date with Zach. Sam sighed happily. "I'll take wild."

By the time Abby and Jo came over, chalk-covered and sweaty, Sam and Stephan had set up four canvas chairs in the shade of the RV's foldout canopy. The guys raised their beers as the women approached. "To our adventurous ladies!" Stephan announced, taking a deep swig.

Jo collapsed into one of the chairs, grinning. "Give me one of those beers, or you will never see me naked again. And a water, because I am a shriveled-up husk of a woman."

Stephan passed her both drinks, and Jo downed an entire water bottle in one long chug before tipping her head back with a sigh. "Fuck yes."

"Me too." Abby gestured. "And please open them, because my hands don't work anymore."

Sam laughed. "That's not fun for any of us, if your hands don't work."

"I have other ways." Grinning impishly, Abby took the bottle of water and guzzled some. "Damn, there is nothing like cold water. My bottle got all hot in the sun." She wiped sweat from her forehead. "I don't know how you can handle this desert heat, Jo. I think I'm cooking, right here in the shade."

"Again. Shriveled-up husk, right here." Jo pointed to herself. "And I grew up with it. It'll get cooler when the sun goes down."

"That reminds me." Abby looked at Sam. "What do you think about camping outside tonight, rather than in the RV? Jo was saying there's a spot not far from here, and we can stay out and look at the stars. We have tents."

Sam tipped his beer to Abby's. "A night under the desert stars? I'm in."

Their camping spot was the picture of seclusion, nestled amid rock formations and the desert expanse. The sun set in a wash of color, bathing their tents and campfire first in purple twilight and then, finally, blue-black darkness. Sam lay back on the blanket, staring up at the stars coming into view. Abby lay beside him, her fingers entwined with his. He heard someone shift nearby, and raised his head to watch Stephan spread their blanket along Abby's other side, and then settle in next to Jo, the four of them side by side, staring up at the stars.

After a few minutes, Abby rolled up onto one elbow, her face temporarily occluding the stars. She smiled down at him, difficult to see in the dim light from their fire, hair tumbling down over her shoulders. She leaned in to kiss him. "I love you."

"I love you, too." He slid an arm around her to pull her closer, deepening the kiss, welcoming her warm weight in the chilly evening air. She curled against him, pillowing her head on his chest, and they stared up at the night sky together. Overhead, the Milky Way painted a purple-colored streak from horizon to horizon, a breathtaking expanse.

They gasped simultaneously as a shooting star lit the night, a crisp slash of brightness that bloomed and faded almost immediately.

"Make a wish," Abby murmured into his ear. She pressed warm against his side, and beyond her, two good friends lay beneath the same tapestry of stars. They might go to bed all together tonight, or separately, and tomorrow was a whole new adventure.

Sam had no need of a wish. He closed his eyes and smiled.

Acknowledgments

Like all books, *Just Past Two* has come to life thanks to many people's input and support. First, I'd like to thank my agent, the indefatigable Saritza Hernandez, who has guided me throughout my writing career and without whom I would surely flounder. Her keen business sensibilities are accompanied by boundless compassion, and I am infinitely grateful for her help.

This book is the end result of two editors as well: Tera Cuskaden, who saw this novel through its infancy, and Heather Howland, who pushed it through its adolescence. It's a very different book than when I first drafted it—it even has a different name—but I'm pleased with the final result, and that is the direct result of editorial feedback and advice. While I may not have known what I was in for at the outset, the final product is worth the struggle, and I appreciate all the input along the way to help this book become the best it can be.

I am beyond lucky to have an incredible network of friends, family, and found-family. Their love and support nurtured me throughout this writing process. A few specific shout-outs: AnneAmanda, for blurb help and honest critique; Kysmet, for tea and life coaching exchanges; Fey Couch Goblin for tough love along with the mushy gross kind; and my husband, he of myriad nicknames, for everything, all the time, forever. I love you all.

About the Author

Elia Winters holds a degree in English Literature and teaches at a small rural high school where she runs too many extracurricular activities. She balances her love of the outdoors with a bottomless well of geekiness; in her spare time, she is equally likely to be found skiing, camping, playing tabletop games, or watching *Doctor Who*. A writer all her life, Elia likes to dabble in many genres, but erotic romance has been one of her favorites since she first began sneaking her mother's romance novels. She currently lives in New England with her loving husband and their odd assortment of pets. Find out more at EliaWinters.com and follow her on Twitter @EliaWinters.

Discover the Comes in Threes series

THREE-WAY SPLIT

Made in United States
Troutdale, OR
12/05/2024

25828323R00135